I0549163

Shadoworld
SHADOW OF THE SUN

MICHEL SAVAGE

www.GreyForest.com

Table of Contents

This is a work of fiction. All the characters and events portrayed in this book are fictitious, and any resemblance to real people or events is purely coincidental.

SHADOWORLD – Shadow of the Sun

The Grey Forest
P.O. Box 71494
Springfield, OR 97475

www.GreyForest.com

Cover art by Tang Yuehui

ISBN: 978-09719168-0-7

1st Edition: July 2002
2nd Edition: Aug 2016
3rd Edition Dec 2025

Printed in the United States of America

0 9 8 7 6 5 4 3

Into the Darkness...

On a distant world, Bronze Age tribes live on an immense planet with an orbit so vast and a rotation so slow that a full planetary day would last a decade. As a result of this, the inhabitants of this world have evolved in such a way that they must continually migrate throughout their lives to avoid the long cold death of nightfall.

Mentioned within are bizarre creatures that men ride as beasts of burden and animals they hunt for food, but the one important difference is the way they tell time; as there is no reference we use such as 'yesterday, today or tomorrow'. Small beads are strung upon a cord and slipped over a knot at the passing of a "day", a completed string is called a 'band', in all senses, nearly equally compared to a calendar month. This is an ancient way of telling time, for hours of the day were not so important as were the planning of the seasons. However, the seasons in this world exist in three global belt zones, that of morning, noon, and sunset, as there is only perpetual day with different tribes that prefer to travel in accustomed regions that journey along the path of the sun as the climate changes. Nearly their entire world is dry land, and nautical travel is unheard of since the few scattered oceans and large lakes contain strange and dangerous beasts, and are thus avoided. Having never seen the night sky, they hold a religious and primal fear of dark shadows and the night.

As of late, there have been disturbing events that have been deeply troubling the inhabitants of this world, revealing evidence perhaps, that something is lurking on the dark side...

Titles by Michel Savage

Faerylands Series
The Grey Forest
Soulstorm Keep
Sorrowblade
Ivory

Shadoworld Series
Shadow of the Sun
Veil of Shadows
Shadows Gate

Outlaws of Europa
Rebels of Alpha Prime

Hellbot • Battle Planet

A Couple of Zeros

Forgotten Future

Broken Mirror

Project EVE

Witchwood

7
৩৩৪

Chapter 1

"Tara! Why are you being so lazy today, finish securing that tent," Torg grumbled.

"Yes father," he answered immediately. Children of the Plains Clan were known for their obedience and respect for tradition, and above all, their elders.

Several members of their tribe had just finished their rest period and were packing up supplies for their journey to the western fjords of the Sorran River, where they met the Cliffs of Chaos. This was the last stretch of many beads of travel, and everyone was looking forward to settling down for the next several bands before the tribe would have to advance to the next settlement.

"Father, how long will it be before we reach the river?" the boy asked, for a large river was a rare sight indeed. Torg tightened the saddle on his barath, which were common riding beasts used by the plainsmen.

"It will only be two beads until we make sight of the Sorran, my son, however, we won't reach camp till the third," his father answered while Tara mounted his barath as the rest of the group finished packing and resumed their long trek.

The plains were pleasantly warm, and Tara couldn't help but fall asleep in the comforting shade of his basket saddle, lying under its woven canopy. The sweet scent of the grass was carried along on a gentle wind. The soft gait of their mounts across the level plains and the music of the bells they wore brought the boy a peaceful nap, with curious dreams of a nightfall he has never seen.

After two beads of travel, their caravan reached the outer tips of the canyons. Running along the top edge, one could see the river far below, the thunder of its waters could be heard echoing from the cliff walls. This was Tara's first time seeing the legendary river, his father's third.

"Father, what is that sound?" Tara asked as they were approaching the end of the plains.

""That is the voice of the Sorran," he smiled, stroking his beard.

"It's as loud as a storm!" the boy exclaimed, his eyes wide with wonder.

"The Sorran is a storm in itself," the chieftain answered as the boy listened intently, "it is said, the river is the lifeblood of our world with waters as blue as the sky but beware the lure it puts in your heart, for the blood of the world gives life to many other creatures who would feed upon your own."

Many of the other young men in the tribe took this potent advice with the assurance that there was hard truth in their chieftain's words; for many have seen the strange creatures that lurk near bodies of water but far fewer men have lived to speak of the nightmares that reside beneath the surface of such rivers and lakes.   There were legendary beasts so enormous that they could swallow an entire caravan whole, and some so small, they could crawl under your skin and eat you alive from the inside. Some monsters were so invisible and silent, that a score of men could be killed and one would suspect nothing until it was too late. Many stories have been told of creatures so horrible that they could kill a man with a glance, by removing his soul and leave their body as nothing more than an empty shell.

One would not put much faith in such exotic tales if the Plainsmen were known for such colorful exaggerations, but they weren't. The old trails were barely visible but well worn from many travelers. Many bands before them, other clans who prefer a much cooler climate, had traversed this very path. Following the long shadows of the land and to always wake to an endless sunrise; Tara had always thought that was a strange way to live.

After scaling the steep paths to the canyon floor, the caravan sighted a suitable place to rest their tired beasts near a small alcove that breached the high cliff walls.

"You can fish along with the other boys as we ready camp farther along the path. You may also bathe in the current of the river, but be wary of still water!" Torg warned his son as he hurried ahead of the caravan to lead the few pack animals which had strayed from the group. Tara watched as his father gathered their reins and led the rest of the caravan to a grove of trees, where the group took shelter under the tall cliff face. The other boys had unpacked several spears and nets and were struggling to untangle them.

"Tara, come help us!" Dayrn, one of the younger boys pleaded as he tried to unwrap a small fishing net alongside a group of dusty and aggravated children pulling on all sides of the tangled web.

Tara ambled towards them in no great hurry while he gazed upward at the great cliff walls in wonder, feeling much smaller under their leaning presence. The boys managed to unravel the net, while a few of the other children and their ever-observant mothers played on the edge of the river. They netted a few fish and gathered a number of plants growing upon the banks.

As long as he could remember, Tara was used to

washing with only a damp cloth and a few cups worth of water, although, immersing himself in the warm river was truly a luxury beyond comparison. While the other children found entertainment in gathering water, berries, and fish; Tara wandered off, entranced by the new sounds of the roaring river and the whistle of the wind through the cliffs that towered above. He jumped from boulder to boulder, exploring every new crack and branch that the maze of narrow clefts broke into.

As he made his way quietly through the tight canyon, he spotted an Aeta, which was a frail-looking but nimble creature, commonly hunted in most parts of this zone. Though, it was odd to see one alone for they usually traveled in herds. Tara watched in silence, admiring the beauty of the creature. The graceful aeta crept up to the water's edge of a small lagoon and drank from the still waters near its shallows.

"There you are!" Dayrn shouted, shattering the perfect tranquility of the moment. The older boy huffed as he climbed up over a boulder and poised behind Tara.

The startled aeta took one glance up at the two children and vaulted away, understandably since Tara, himself, nearly jumped out of his pants from being equally surprised. Unfortunately for the startled animal, it had bolted directly into the lagoon.

The animal kicked and splashed and was now up to its neck in the deep pond, as it clearly didn't know how to swim. Tara was afraid the delicate animal would drown, however, it would receive no such mercy. The poor creature, realizing it had no place to go, turned back towards the shore and had made it halfway to safety when the alarm in its eyes flared into one of stark terror.

Its primal scream made a terrible sound as a mass of

oblong fish attached to its body like glistening green locks of hair. The suction fish swarmed over the poor creature. It struggled as it tried to reach the shore but its strength was literally drained from its body. As it scraped a few of the parasites from its neck in vain, streams of blood sprayed into the blue water from these wounds; turning it a foaming red as the full fury of hundreds of the swarming fish fixated on their prey.

The doomed creature slowly ceased its struggling. The little green fish now covered its entire body from head to hoof. It fell over and floated in the water, like an enormous ball of squirming moss, then slowly sank below. The dark ripples of water quickly settled and a peaceful calm returned to the quiet lagoon. The two boys stood for long moments staring wide-eyed in horror, for now, only a patch of dark water near the shore and their knowledge of the nightmare that lay feeding just below its surface could cast a shadow upon the deceptive beauty of the still lake.

Neither of them said a word to each other as they turned and quickly made their way back to camp. They were not so much in a hurry to reach the others, as they were to escape the terrible scene they had just witnessed moments before.

After a clan banquet consisting of local fruits and fish, all the men of the camp planned their hunt after getting their rest. The clan would be staying in this area for a short spell, and sleep shifts were at leisure. When Tara was excited to mention that he had spotted an aeta, Dayrn swiftly elbowed Tara in the ribs and shot him a dirty look to hush. Both boys then began to fear being scolded for wandering off earlier. After being questioned by his father about his story, Tara admitted his whereabouts and the area where he spotted the unfortunate creature.

"The young animal was attacked by a swarm of strange fish in the lagoon," he added unwillingly.

"What color where these fish?" Torg asked with an even temper, though seemingly not angry with the boys.

"They were a deep green and shaped like a hollow cane. There were hundreds of them," he exclaimed while showing their size with the breadth of his hands.

"Hmm, as I feared. You two were very lucky, those were gut leeches, but I am troubled about your description as such leeches are usually very light in color and I have never seen one larger than a man's finger," his father mentioned as he gazed into the flickering fire.

Tara held a new respect for his father. He, like Dayrn, had expected to be publicly scolded but his father had only shown concern for their safety in his words.

"Tara, you will lead us to this lagoon before the hunting party begins. Get some rest now, as we have much to do, especially if you are to join us for the hunt afterward," his father advised.

Tara smiled and was a little stunned. Not only was he to play guide but he had also been invited to join the other men for their hunting trip. Things were getting exciting, even for a boy his age. Torg lay down in his tent and slipped another bead over the knot of the calendar loop hanging from his belt. Another few, and the band would be complete. It had been a long time since the death of his wife. He thought how proud she would be of her son and how quickly he was growing up. He whispered a silent prayer to her and looked out into the bright orb of the sun high above, where she waited for him; so was his belief.

When Tara finally awoke, the camp was in a bustle.

The tribesmen were oiling bowstrings and sharpening their spears, and a few were enjoying a much-needed bath they had missed before. A majority of the men stayed behind to feed and care for their pack animals while their Chief, and a few others, followed Tara along the banks of the river. Even at their quick pace it took them a while to reach the lagoon, where they keep well clear of the water's edge.

"Tara, is this where the small animal was attacked?" the Chieftain inquired.

His son nodded. The chieftain picked up what looked to be a large shriveled branch from the bank. It was one of the huge gut leeches, having been flung to the shore in the death throes of the aeta. Powerless while out of the water, it had dried out and was now quite dead. Torg peered through it as though it were a hollow twig.

"This one is enormous! Usually, only one or two leeches are capable of entering the body, where they must be dug out, but a swarm as you mentioned," nodding to his son, "...has never been heard of before," his father declared while he passed around the stiff dead leech for the other men to gawk at.

One tribesman retraced the tracks of the aeta from the shoreline. Their small group elected to continue onward, for it would be a stroke of luck if there were actually a herd of them nearby. Tracking prey in the soft sand was an easy task for these Plainsman. After the endless wanderings of the animal, they discovered its prints had emerged from the mouth of a small cave. The men paused and looked at each other in mild surprise.

"Aeta have never been cave-dwellers, this must lead somewhere beyond the cliffs," one of the men stated. They gathered dry brush and dead branches from the scarce trees near the cave entrance, and fashioned a handful of makeshift torches. It had been a long time since they left the camp, but they had come this far; and if a baby aeta could brave a journey through the grotto, by damn, they could as well.

Tara kept in the middle of the group, for this was not only his first time exploring a cave, but also his first true experience of being plunged into complete darkness. A few adults noticed Tara's anxiety as he peered over his shoulder towards the crack of fading daylight they left behind, and they shared his feeling of dread.

The passage was narrow and it was a strange sensation to feel the cool rock against his hands. Many of the men were sharing the same thoughts and hurried along for fear that their torches might burn out while they were still trapped within. Water could be heard rushing through the cavern, breaking the eerie silence. The tunnel opened into a large sculpted room with enormous stalactites dripping as they formed into liquid stone. One of the tribesmen ventured towards an underground stream where he found that the waters were painfully cold to the touch.

"This is freshwater, an extension of the river above," he aired. The group passed on, for the torches they brought were few in number and burned far faster than they preferred. An eerie silence passed between them as they wandered through a large chamber filled with still pools lying beside their path. Small bone-white creatures could be seen slithering within their shallow waters.

"I think I see a light ahead," one of the men shouted while rushing forward in his zeal to escape the confines of the cave. His is elation was shared by more than a few of their men as they scuttled eagerly towards the shaft of sunlight piercing the end of the tunnel.

They climbed up through a small crack of sunlight, scraping their backs and shoulders in their eagerness to escape the embrace of darkness. They found a canyon lying beyond, maintaining a healthy valley that spread out before them. A branch of the Sorran River could be heard thundering in the distance, echoing from the surrounding cliffs.

"Look here! There are many aeta prints and spattered blood among the cave entrance. It appears that a herd was here, likely fleeing from a predator and became trapped in this alcove, but only the young aeta was small enough to enter this cavern and found a way out on the other side," their scout mentioned while examining the soil as he read the marks left behind.

"I concur," stated one of the men solemnly, "I only hope that this predator you mentioned is smaller than me!" he barked while flexing his muscles as the others chuckled alongside him.

It was good to laugh away the shivers that the cave had brought to their bones. To be trapped in complete darkness was a nightmare they had all secretly feared. The valley was quite small and they explored it in hopes of finding the herd, though none of the warriors cherished the idea of dragging a dead animal carcass back through the narrow tunnels of the cave.

"A score of them came through here not long ago, maybe two beads ago, maybe sooner," one of the older trackers said as he sifted through the animal droppings.

In the middle of the small valley they came upon a most curious site; at the edge of a large natural spring stood a monolith of golden stones forming a massive archway over the site.

"What do you think this is?" Torg asked.

"Who knows, I've never seen anything like it. This structure must have been built by members of the mountain clans, only they can work stone like this," one of the tribesmen added while inspecting the smooth yellow marble.

Their group took shade under the structure as a few of the other men refilled their water skins at the spring, one of them arrived back with a crushed aeta skull.

"I found several animal limbs at the edge of the cliff over there," he mentioned while pointing off towards the narrow edge of the valley, "it appeared as if the animals were torn apart limb by limb. Only a large pack of Vangees could go through a herd like that. They left a real mess behind and there is still a lot of meat rotting on the carcasses."

Vangees were a real menace, Tara had only seen one before in his lifetime, and that particular beast had already been killed. The vile creatures were nearly the size of a full-grown man and covered in thick fur, while their snouts were adorned with jagged razor-sharp beaks. It was said they were nothing but lone scavengers, although they were occasionally known to hunt in packs of a dozen or more. They were such horridly unclean and foul-smelling beasts that even their furs were good for nothing and were usually burned because of their awful stench.

"I doubt that it was vangees," his comrade cut in, "those repulsive creatures are very thorough and would have cleaned every bone to its nub. Besides, I didn't see any of their tracks, and those filthy beasts would have left some evidence of their droppings behind," he motioned with his hand to the sky, "Furthermore, I have never heard of vangees ever roaming in the noonday zone!"

"He's right; those beasts only thrive in the twilight of nightfall. They prefer to hunt the weak and conceal themselves in the shadows," one of the elders affirmed.

"Perhaps so," the man finally admitted, "but look here, those wild animals didn't do this!" he said while holding up the crushed aeta skull. Inspecting it closely, it was clear that someone had carefully sawed off the horns from its crest and made several intricate decorative carvings into the skull itself. None of them had ever seen craftwork of its kind before, "I found this lying in the dirt just beyond this strange archway."

They all looked at one another in confusion. It was very interesting and extremely delicate work, the artisan must have been very skilled indeed. The engraved patterns seemed to weave upon itself. It was too bad the skull had been shattered or it might have been worth something in value for trade.

Then again, they began to wonder why or even how men of the mountain clans had transported such massive stone blocks into the middle of the valley floor. Apparently, the structure was a flagstone to mark the location of the water spring but where had they gotten these strange marble blocks? Certainly not from anywhere nearby, as there was no quarry within sight. The strata of the surrounding cliffs was plainly peppered with gray and white stone, and there were no roads or posted tracks into or out of this valley except by the way they had just arrived through the small cavern rift; where no mountain clansman could possibly travel as they were far larger in stature than normal men.

They all made their way back to the spring by the marbled arch as a few of the men washed their muddied tunics in the shallow waters. The small river was swift, which made it safe to use as there were very few, if any, harmful water-breathers that lived in such currents, and most were so small you could hold them in your hands.

A number of the men got their wits about them and agreed it would be too strenuous to carry back any aeta they might find back to their encampment. They had come too far and there was no chance of getting a barath through the narrow cleft into the cavern to carry the burden for them, let alone the tall boulders they had traversed just to get to the lagoon itself. They assembled together, and the hunters mutually agreed to abandon this short jaunt and return back to camp.

Just as they were finalizing their decision, a disturbing sound could be heard echoing from the valley walls; a noise resembling the shrieking of a dozen screaming women, but this dreadful sound was far more terrifying. None of them had heard anything like it before, and the men had no idea what it could be. They glanced at one another, startled. It certainly wasn't vangees they heard howling but *whatever* it was, might well likely be what had killed the entire herd of wild aeta.

As the strange shrieks echoed through the valley, everyone quickly agreed it was time to return to the home camp immediately. They back-tracked their steps in haste and were nearly to the cave entrance when everyone suddenly picked up their pace. Tara could not see why they were running now but got a much better view of the situation when his father hastily launched his son upon his broad shoulders and continued his sprint for the cave entrance.

There was something very large and reptilian turning the bend and was quickly closing upon their position.

Bouncing along on his father's shoulders, Tara could see that the monstrosity had the identical coloring of the surrounding cliffs and was also quite massive in size. Its head and jaws were wide and its body covered in thick scales. Tara could not tell how many legs it had, maybe six, maybe more.

It screeched again, but this time its cry was painful to their ears. The cave entrance was near, but unfortunately, so was the enormous beast. The men headed straight for the cave mouth at the end of the alcove. Tara noticed that for some reason, the lizard creature clung to the cliffside and never ventured from it; for it would have certainly caught their group had it abandoned the cliff wall and rushed them straight on upon the valley floor.

Plainsmen hunters were skilled trackers, but perhaps that's why they couldn't tell what had decimated the wild herd. This monster had not been traversing the ground to leave any tracks of its passage, for it had been moving along the steep canyon walls. The boy couldn't figure out how this giant creature kept itself vertical on the cliffside, for one would think its sheer weight alone would cause it to come crashing to the ground.

Tara was one of the first to fly in through the entrance when they reached the alcove as his father launched him through to the safety of the cave. The fear of escaping the beast was suddenly replaced by being dropped into the stark blackness of the grotto. Tara's eyes were unable to adjust to the sudden darkness and he only prayed that someone still had a torch or two left to use.

The creature could be heard screaming and struggling to fit its enormous head into the narrow alcove just outside the mouth of the cave. The rest of the men scurried in, bowling each other over in their haste to escape the horrid beast. Large plumes of dust covered them as the monster huffed and screeched again, causing them to go momentarily deaf. Then one of the men shrieked in horror as a huge forked tongue slithered through the cave entrance and scored his side. The creature's tongue was designed to stick and wrap around its prey but was thwarted by the dust it had layered upon their bodies only moments before.

All of the men backed up against the walls to escape its reach. Torg and a few others turned their spears upon the flailing tongue, but their aim was poor in the darkness and they risked the chance of skewering their fellow man. The beast withdrew its tongue and screeched again, seemingly more distant this time; though no one dared to peek through the entrance to verify that claim.

Luckily, one of the younger men still had a few torches strapped to his back. Using them sparingly, their group hurried back through the cavern. Due to the lack of adequate light, a younger fellow in the rear slipped on the wet rocks and into one of the still pools, where he screamed like a toddler as the small albino snakes slithered over him. He was quickly extracted and only began to quiet down when he had felt neither a bite nor sting; but was merely covered in thick coats of dripping slime.

Their group was a sight to see when they wandered back into camp. In alarm, a few of the elders grabbed for their war spears as their own clansmen approached, as they were entirely unrecognizable; for they were all covered from head to toe in fine gray dust from their jaunt through the cave. After the commotion of their arrival died down and put at ease, the men got cleaned up and the women of the clan took the task of tending to those that were injured. Understandably, their hunting party was canceled until much later as the men involved were too exhausted to do anything but rest. All except for Tara, of course, who stayed up and told the rest of the children about their grand adventure at least half a dozen times; and naturally, each retelling of his tale was more colorful and exaggerated than the last.

Everyone agreed the lone lagoon and the caverns were now strictly off limits to the children; especially so to Tara and Dayrn, who were prone to exploring without parental permission. As time passed at the seasonal camp, a few of the boys of age were being taught how to hunt and how to fashion their own spears. They would be allowed to carry them as a symbol of honor when they made their first kill. Embarrassingly, Tara's spear sat alone for many beads until he improved the strength of his arm and the accuracy of his aim.

When the chieftain addressed the circle of boys during one hunting lesson, he tutored them into reciting the ancient laws of their tribe.

"Not only will your kill feed yourself, but also all of your clan," Torg mentioned, "We are all family," which was the customary chant of the Plains Tribes, for life was too harsh to survive alone in this world.

Tara carried his new war spear with him everywhere until he realized it was actually a bit cumbersome to be doing so all the time, especially for daily life at camp. It was hard to let go of his new symbol of status, for ego and pride had filled his head; why else would the grown clansmen smirk when they passed him by?

The Cliffs of Chaos extended for many miles. Their own encampment was near its mouth, where the Sorran erupted from an underground spring in a flurry of mist and rainbows of light that danced in the sky above. Their stay here had lasted many bands. One of the women had given birth, and a few of the adolescents had achieved their ritual spears and hunting rights with their clan. Torg painted pictographs on the cliff walls for the following sunset tribes who used this road, to warn them of the treacherous lagoon and the hidden valley, and of the devilish beast that dwelled beyond the cave.

It would soon be time to move onward to the north, where the weather was much cooler but the arc of their path in this stretch of the land was the only trail through the vast chain of mountains ahead. There would be little rest for the tribesmen until they reached the great stone settlements, which were built over hundreds of lifetimes by their forefathers. They were massive cities abandoned to the darkness until the distant sunrise warmed their walls again in the long-awaited dawn. It was within these immense markets where the divergent tribes met, where goods were traded, stories were told, and new husbands or wives found mates and joined other clans, taking on new paths of their own.

Torg wondered if there would be a day his own son would take up his mantle and lead his clan, or perhaps his boy would decide to transfer to another tribe, should he so choose. The grand city of Hagda was Tara's birthplace, and his son would be one cycle old when they reached it. He looked out over the Sorran river's wide blue waters and out to the horizon beyond.

'How fast they grow up,' he thought to himself.

Chapter 2

Reaching the city of Hagda would take nearly two bands traveling through the twisting valleys. The mountain passes were shorter but fraught with danger, and baraths were not exactly the most preferable mounts for negotiating such rocky terrain. The mountain tribes used beasts called Rorns, which were much more accustomed to such steep trails and were well adapted as excellent climbers, but Torg was neither familiar with the mountain paths nor were rorns easy to come by, for the mountain clans would refuse to part with them cheaply.

The Plains Clan had packed enough dried fish and fruits to last them for a term, though hunting while passing through the northern valleys would be necessary to survive the long journey to Hagda. In areas along the canyon walls, Torg had read pictographs describing the conditions of the earlier tribes but he could not quite decipher the entire message.

"Some tribal leaders can't draw properly," he mumbled to himself in aggravation, "can anyone make out what this says?" he asked his clansmen while several of the men gathered to examine the etchings.

"It seems to me like some type of structure was taken down," Torg suggested, pointing at the image.

"*Humph*! It looks as if they were trying to say an entire village was destroyed," Dooroo, the grand elder of their clan exclaimed. No one could deny that was the way it appeared, but nobody could believe that anyone would do such a thing. Perhaps it was the fierce seasonal storms which were responsible for the destruction.

When cloudfronts from the dark side passed into the warm rays of the sun, sudden and violent storms have been witnessed to last many bands without weakening. Tara inquired about these so-called morning tribes.

"The dawn tribes are all clans that travel ahead of us," Torg schooled his son, "some of the Mountain, Snow, Forest, and even Desert Clans. They may prefer cooler weather but I also hear that trees bear more fruit in that climate and that the ground is richer in moisture, which makes farming easier," he stated.

"But what of the Valley Clans, father?" the boy questioned.

"Those from the valleys are a strange group, Tara, and most tribes avoid them," his father relayed with disgust.

"But, why?" the inquisitive boy asked brightly as he brought his mount up to stride beside his father.

"Some clans have unusual customs, Tara, and not all are truly understood or accepted. Some even speak in a different language, pierce their tongues and faces, and even paint their whole bodies and wear masks," he stated.

"All of the time?" the boy asked, wide-eyed.

"Yes, for every waking moment, I hear. Once I was in the city of Cerizel with Dooroo," Torg stated as Tara turned back to see the old gray-haired man nod towards his father, "...and a valley tribe arrived, creating a wild ruckus. Their whole caravan was adorned with such colors that they looked like a festival all to themselves. They brought many feathered masks, strange hides, and exotic jewelry to trade but it was shortly understood that they only traveled so far north because there was a shortage of wild game to be found in the valleys as a result of excessive storms and floods afflicting the southern regions at the time," as they reached the end of the canyons, the roaring of the river softly died away and his father continued, "The people of the valley clan were rude. They would pass you by as though you didn't exist, pushing their way through crowds and threatening others who resisted them. Even the great warriors of the forest tribes cowered when confronted by them, out of fear of their witchcraft," Torg mentioned, describing the great size of the Forest giants, "there were relatively few women in their group, and they traded enormous sums to try to sway new blood to join their clan but they weren't very successful. Few decent women would ever consider consorting with the likes of them. One season, a group of Valley tribesmen were caught trying to kidnap several women from another tribe, and as a result, their entire clan was exiled from the city," Torg remarked.

Dooroo approached Tara while attempting to sound overly dramatic with his cracked and rusty voice.

"The forest warriors would not even touch the people of the valley clan for fear of being tainted with the spirits they are said to possess. Some even say they eat other people," he remarked as Tara cringed, "...others say they are soulless, and paint their bodies to hide their decaying flesh that lies rotting beneath."

Tara tried to get comfortable so he could rest during his ride to the northern mountains. His mind raced with fanciful visions of the tales he was told, but now he wanted nothing more than to actually see the wild men of the Valley tribe, at least once in his lifetime.

The trip north to the western edge of the Charred Mountains was uneventful until a group of children noticed a Sprig, which was a rare type of tree that slowly moves in a strange way. The unique shrub cannot exist without sunlight, so such plants must also migrate as any other living creature. It progressed much slower than their caravan, of course, however, it did not tire. Sighting one is considered a sign of good fortune.

The woven carts of the plains people are shaped like shells, and catching a moment of sleep while traveling by wagon or mount was common practice. Baraths also have the ability to slumber as they walk, trotting along in a daze, but must be slapped awake whenever they should wander off path. Riders and mounts alike have been known to run over cliffs without missing a stride because both rider and mount had fallen asleep. Only attentive caravan masters could prevented such misfortune.

The Charred Mountains were well described, as their soil was a dark shade of black and held much native vegetation that was colored in dark tones. It was said that long ago the sun came down to take up a holy man at this very spot, and thus, burned the whole mountain where it had touched. One of the elders mentioned that the weather had turned quite strange, for the sky to the north turned a creamy orange while murky clouds drifted lazily before it. The elder mentioned the only time he had seen such a sight before was when a violent wind funnel struck. Even though the strange haze was still a ways in the distance their current path, unfortunately, led straight into its folds. The chief discussed the situation with the other men of the tribe.

"We can camp here until the skies ahead clear but that will cut short our stay at Hagda," the elder proclaimed.

"Perhaps the clouds are moving west, and to stop now would only hamper our efforts to clear the northern pass ...damn these cursed mountains!" another clansman remarked.

"If we can outrun the storm before it reaches the

northern tip of the pass, then we should be clear to reach the city," another man added his voice.

"This is foolish, we are only assuming that the storm is heading towards us, we should just continue on," one of the herdsmen debated.

"Agreed, to falter now could be devastating if we were caught in such a storm with the mountains between us and the nearest city," the Chief admitted.

"I say the walking tree was a divine omen, and that we should continue onward," the herdsman advised.

"*Humph...*" the elder scoffed back at him with a grunt.

"We should outpace the storm, are we agreed?" Torg finally suggested as the other men conceded in unison.

The unusual squall turned out to be more distant than was first thought and it slowly faded away towards the east of their given path. Weather among the plains was fairly predictable and massive storms such as the one they had witnessed were exceptionally rare. Luckily, they encountered a herd of horned Grags, which provided fresh meat for their group, as the dried fish and shriveled water fruit they had in stock were starting to go stale. Berry bushes were common at the northern fork and the womenfolk gathered basketfuls from the side of the path. Many overindulged on this treat and it was discovered they had a mildly intoxicating effect, which nobody really complained about.

A roar could be heard in the distance, it was the Trygot River branching from the Oran Sea. The ocean was avoided because of its lack of vegetation, though it held a substantial amount of wildlife and an even stranger aquatic animals. It was said that entire tribes have disappeared there with nothing but their carts, wagons, and baskets left scattered upon its quiet shores, as if whole caravans had been swept up and pulled into its bitter waters.

At the northern post of the trail, they crossed more disturbing news. The pictographs they found there included the rarely seen figures of the Snow Tribes. Apparently, they were traveling to Hagda this cycle as well. Many of the mountain tribes described the same vandalism of their villages and forts. This was a mystery indeed. The journey from the northern fork to Hagda seemed very short, although their provisions were now getting low and many of the men blamed the shortage of available wild game on the uncommonly high number of travelers who had passed this way before them.

The city of Hagda was a magnificent sight at a distance, standing as an immense circle of stone buildings and intricate towers. It was one of the largest cities ever built, matched only by the exotic forums of Silistra, cradled near the lush valleys of Torru. Hagda was a merchant's paradise, and with so many new clans meeting at one time it was sure to be packed to the brim.

"We may have trouble finding a space of our own," Dooroo mentioned.

"I'm sure there will be room, old fellow, even for the likes of you," Torg laughed as the rest of the company chuckled along with him, while Dooroo flashed a frown and a furrowed brow at his chieftain's jest.

The gates of the city were massive and were guarded by giant forest warriors that were nearly twice the size of an average man in stature. Bandit tribes were uncommon, as they usually avoided cities but a visual deterrent to keep such marauders at bay was well justified. Torg stated his Clans purpose and length of stay to the city guards, and in return, their Chief was informed that all clan leaders were to meet at the oval tower in ten beads time and was promptly presented with a special pass for the occasion. Apparently, the meeting was crucial enough that they didn't want any clan chiefs to miss this important assembly.

As they entered into the city, exotic and overbearing odors of incense, spices, and cooked meats, filled the narrow streets of the marketplace. Torg led his group to the edge of the city where they found a handful of vacant huts stationed with a water trough for their mounts. Their immediate neighbors were one of the rare Snow clan tribes, who all appeared as if they weren't exactly enjoying the pleasantly warm weather of the noon season. They only wore loincloths and immersed themselves with water from the nearby well more often than naught. Their pale white mounts were large and very furry, which also seemed to be in a grouchy mood at all times in this climate.

Their speech was a little odd, but their children played happily with the other tribal youths and were actually quite friendly. Tara was told only to leave their camp with the other adults of their clan, for the city was so large that it would be easy for a lone child to get lost. Most of the single men in the group cleaned up after unsaddling and attending their mounts, and took straight away to seeking women of questionable character.

Tara noticed most of the children from the snow tribe wore small tusks in their ears and adorned tattoos upon their foreheads. He discovered that when they dressed up tightly in their furs, that their people all pretty much looked the same, and as such, it was only their unique facial tattoos that allowed them to recognize one another. One of the older boys offered to give him a tattoo, but

Tara chose to ask his father's permission prior.

Forced to accompany the group of their elderly women was not exactly what Tara would have preferred, but he could see how wandering off alone in such a crowd could be dangerous. They kept him busy holding baskets full of fruits and pelts which the women made him carry. He found one peddler who let him pet his exotic animals who were soft and furry, some scaly and vibrant, and some that could change color right before your eyes. It was delightful and amusing to have them climb onto his shoulders and atop his head, when they were so inclined.

Tara felt bad when he returned to camp, since it seemed he had somehow lost his belt knife during his trip into the marketplace. His father would certainly not be pleased, as tools and weapons were not easy to come by. Many of the men returned with wineskins full of ale, while a few others were hired for work to repair parts of the city in return for payment of sweetmeats and herbs. Most of their journeys to the market were for curiosity but the well-fashioned spears that the Plainsmen crafted and traded, allowed their people a decent living while staying within the vast walls of this bustling city.

On one particular outing, Tara and the other children accompanied the adults to a large shrine covered with colorful tarps. Within its center was a large fountain with a platform at the top, upon which musicians played with drums, and flutes, and various stringed instruments. Several women danced around in their veils and decorated robes, while even a few of the children joined in. There were so many festivals held everywhere in the city that no one person could possibly see them all.

During the celebration, while eagerly gnawing on some flatbread and a leg of glazed meat, Tara noticed a shapely young girl wearing something like a cat mask, swaying to the rhythm of the music. Apparently she had her attention on him. At first, he thought she might be from a valley tribe from the stories he had heard but she was only wearing common veils, and her body was not covered with paint and tattoos as was commonly rumored. Mesmerized, he watched as she dared to come closer. She struck out with a knife at the roast in front of him, plucked it off the silver tray, and took a savage bite, smiling at him while she chewed upon the meat. Tara glared at the girl and grabbed her arm at the wrist.

"Hey! That's *my* knife!" he shouted, recognizing the blade through all the grease.

"I know dummy," she chuckled, pulling from his grasp with a twist of her wrist; "...I borrowed it from you while you were petting the lockras."

"The what? ...You *borrowed*!" Tara snapped angrily.

"The animals you were petting in the marketplace, that's what they're called, dummy," she grinned as she slipped off her mask. Tara was infuriated, borrowed indeed. He wanted to yell back at her but the words were caught in his throat at the sight of her beauty. Truly, she was quite exceptional, with dark entrancing eyes.

"I was going to give it back," she smirked.

He reached for his knife again but she pulled away once more, hiding it behind her back. He reached behind her, first to the left, then to the right. She was toying with him, and now had him exactly where she wanted.

"*Oooh*, friendly aren't we?" She teased with a smile as they met nose to nose with his arms around her.

Tara pulled away, partly embarrassed, as she graciously handed him back the small knife. Although, he was a tad reluctant to pull away at that moment, for she smelled of incense and sweet oils, and something primal stirred within him. She reached for his free arm and pulled him back into her embrace.

"My name is Lela..." she mentioned, though seemingly reluctant to say more as she looked away coyly.

"Of uh ...of what clan?" Tara inquired nervously, having never been this close to a girl like her before. The girl paused momentarily, appearing uncertain how to respond to his question, "What's wrong?" the boy asked.

"I'm from one of the mountain clans; there are four of them in the city now ...it's just that I've noticed some clans tend not to mix with others," Lela replied.

"Don't be silly," Tara smirked, "many tribes mingle to trade goods and to find new mates," he began to blush, realizing what he had just said aloud a little too late. Lela just flashed him a humorous smile in return.

The gypsy girl offered him a flask of wine and he sneaked a sip with guilt but it appeared the adults were all entertaining themselves with the music and the feast, and not being altogether timid with the ale themselves.

Tara enjoyed Lela's company as the festival waned on. She seemed likely to be slightly older than him but he didn't mind that so much. Her long black hair was braided with an array of decorative coins and golden beads, and her light gauze robes were slightly revealing. They smiled and laughed at each other, sharing their past travels and making jokes about the eccentric elders in their clans. Suddenly, a shout echoed throughout the room and the music abruptly stopped as everyone turned to see a group of forest giants barge into the tent, looking very angry indeed.

Chapter 3

The largest of the giants possessed roughly chiseled features and sported a short gray beard that matched his tussled hair. He, like his companions, wore strange green armor constructed of woven leather, wood, and metal. The graybeard spoke towards the crowd with a deep thundering voice.

"Don't mind us good people, we are simply trying to find an associate of ours, of whom, we were informed, may be among your guests at this establishment," he finished, ending with a most incriminating smile.

The rest of his large companions surrounded the group within the room as they searched every nook and cranny. Out of the corner of his eye, Tara noticed a gentleman in red silk pants bolt upright suddenly, abandoning a most comfortable position he had been enjoying for some time laying among the pillows with ample wine and women within reach. He was apparently trying to make a speedy departure but was promptly apprehended; grasped by the scruff of his neck by one of the large giants before he could even turn around. Graybeard approached as his fellow clansman held their captured prize aloft with his feet dangling in the air off the floor.

"Ador, my old friend, we were beginning to think you didn't like us," he insisted with sedated mirth, "sit, join us for a while," he gestured to the giant who was throttling the poor man, who suddenly dropped him back into the pile of pillows. Their comrades snatched huge platters of meat along with several tankards of mead and joined their leader. The poor little man, for being apparently unharmed, looked quite shaken.

"I was, ah ...was going to look for you, ah ...after the festival, Groheem," he stuttered.

"Oh, I'm sure you were, Ador," the giant smiled while patting a massive hand upon the man's shoulder, the effect of which looked quite painful, "...but, um, after *which* festival, hmm? You know, we haven't seen you for many beads now."

The man's eyes darted nervously, "I, uh, you see..."

"No need to worry, little man, you have found your old friends again! Perhaps we should conclude our business now in case we should lose each other again in this large and crowded city, where you have already slipped away numerous times before," Groheem suggested with a grin.

"Yes, it would be easy to get lost among these narrow streets," one of the fellow giants added with a glare.

"*Poof*! Some people disappear into thin air, and are never seen nor heard from again," another added with a mocking tone while overacting a look of being mystified. The little man's face turned quite pale at his words, especially so compared to his vivid red pants. The Chieftain put his melon size head next to his.

"Where is it?" he quietly breathed while eye to eye with his captive, but the rest of their conversation faded into the noise of the crowd as the musicians continued to play, while the dancers attempted to avoid the group of large warriors altogether. Though, on a few occasions, the serving women had drastically miscalculated the giant's reach, and were frequently man-handled. Tara could see across the fire pit that the little man in red looked quite unhappy seated among his new hosts. Seeing this, Lela managed to pull his attention away.

"Those are forest warriors, and they don't like people

nosing in on their business," she whispered in warning.

"Will they hurt him?" Tara inquired.

"Not likely," she said while passing him another cup of wine, "…if someone has made a promise or bond they cannot fulfill, the giants usually draft them into slavery for a length of time."

"That's barbaric!" Tara shot back.

"Not as barbaric as killing them for failing to keep their word," Lela compromised while she flashed a reluctant smile back at him.

The troop of giants soon left with their newfound acquaintance and the revelry of the party returned to its original vigor. From then on, both Lela and Tara spent much more time in each other's company. They explored the markets together, where Lela acquired by her sleight of hand, a measure of snacks for them to eat, including a few other glittering baubles and knickknacks that happened to slip within her reach. There were numerous temples, shrines, and mazes of streets where the young pair saw many curious beasts, exotic characters, and countless stalls bearing amazing handicrafts of the likes he had never seen before.

The plainsmen were known for their specialized art at making decorative baskets and deadly spears. The valley tribes peddled their masks, exotic herbs, and exquisite pottery. The forest giants hawked their soft furs and hides they trapped. The mountain clans made assorted cheeses and sweet wines of every color and shade. The Desert people created fabric, beads, and delicately crafted jewelry of rubies and gold. In turn, it appeared that the snow tribes made little but finely etched blades made of horn and bones. These they usually traded with the mountain clans who also mined metals, and would craft both bone and steel into fantastic weapons.

The members of the snow tribes had also mentioned they built boats, but who in their right mind would ever sail the vast open waters? Valley tribes had made smaller vessels like canoes to make traveling easier while negotiating rivers, but doing so was risky, and more often than naught, they were lost along with its crew to either turbulent rapids or bizarre beasts that live in the waters depths of solitary lagoons. Fishing by net within a shallow stream was fairly safe, but to get into a flimsy canoe in deep water and chance being eaten alive or drowned was considered an act of lunacy by most.

Torg's clan had managed to trade for many soft pelts, smoked meats, dried spices, and metal ore for their spears. There was relatively little violence in the city, and numerous ceremonies were held for trading brides and grooms amongst the clans. Each tribe made parades to exhibit their talents and frequently argued over different customs and beliefs they held. Many men entertained the customs of the desert tribesmen who sported a number of wives. In turn, a few males had dared the attempt to introduce this dubious practice into their own clan, that is, until they mentioned this ideology to the females of their clans, where their aims towards such carnal desires for possessing harems abruptly withered under their harsh glares.

Maps and new trade routes were posted for all the Clan Chiefs to acquire. Tara learned to play a small clay flute fashioned with a string that he wore around his neck. Lela continued to 'borrow' more things than she paid for, and Tara was sure that she would run into trouble sometime, but didn't fail to notice that these lewd merchants preferred to keep their eyes on the ripe curves of her body, rather than her wandering hands.

Tara was convinced he could not possibly accomplish the same feats of brazen thievery that she got away with, but it did teach him to keep his eyes open.

The time came for the assembly of leaders at the grand tower. The great oval tower was constructed from pale ivory marble and crafted with intricate carvings. The door to the citadel was forged of gilded gold displaying a large sculpture of the sun at its peak. Lamps filled with fragrant oils lit the interior and the floor was wrought of colorful mosaic tiles that brought the shrine to life. Now inside, Torg was beginning to feel a little underdressed.

As he entered, it appeared the courtyard at its center was jammed with hundreds of men and women in splendid garb that were usually only worn for special ceremonies, in an obvious attempt to flaunt their status.

An elder of the forest tribes was the spokesman for this meeting. He was dressed in traditional velvet green robes covered with decorative gold and silver leaves. Strangely, his stature was not as exaggerated as were the other forest tribesmen that were present. The tile floor of the room was ornamented to resemble flames reaching out from a celestial sun, its bright colors weaving and stretching to the edge of the chamber walls. At its center, a circle of glowing gold reflected light from the lanterns. It was upon this rich dais that the elder stood. There was the deep resounding knell of a gong and the chatter of the crowd slowly died away. Finally, the High Elder spoke.

"Many of you see new faces among us in this room. We have here tribes of distant clans, who would rarely visit this city, have done so this cycle but their presence is not merely for trade or commerce, for they bring us a dire warning!" The room immediately erupted with a mixture of subdued chatter at these words. He calmly implored them all into silence once again and motioned towards the large tarp that lay before his feet.

"There have been many reports this last cycle that villages, temples, and forts have been vandalized. This was proven not to be the result of storms, and the damage is so great and widespread that suspicion of this being the work of bandits has been eliminated. For as you know, bandits require other honest tribes to trade so they may rob their spoils; and to destroy that ability with such wanton destruction would fail to benefit them in any form, akin to severing of their own hands." At that, two men came forward and began to lift the tarp, gently revealing what lay beneath, "We have been assured the damage was not done by any of the Valley tribes, and I have come to believe the solemn word of their elders," he continued as numerous masked leaders of the decorative Valley clans among the assembly grunted in approval.

"These items were found among the ruins," he pointed as the tarp was fully unveiled, "any among you who would know of their origins, please be heard."

A few members of the crowd moved in to get a better view while hushed whispers drifted about the room. Torg, himself, was mystified. Held aloft for all to see was a huge pitch-black blade, fashioned from a flat glossy stone. Its handle was crudely constructed of raw wood and leather, apparently with little skill. There was also what appeared to be a chisel with a thick head, made of the same curious obsidian stone, its wide tip broken off from the length of its shaft.

Sitting behind it was the skeleton of a water beast, its huge skull was the length of many men and beheld several rows of sharp jagged teeth. There was also a unusual scaled hide with numerous odd symbols painted upon it. A few leaders of the mountain tribes came forward to handle the strange collection.

"We do much mining across the lands, and would suggest this appears to be some type of chisel for carving stonework," he mentioned, while handling the broken artifact while another of the mountain leaders took up the large black blade to examine it closer.

"These remains of the water-breather was the smallest of hundreds of bones that were discovered," the high elder confessed while pointing towards the sun-bleached skeleton, "...these items were found on dry land a mere three beads journey south of the holy Ottay Shrine. This shrine is not near any source of water that could possibly sustain such mammoth beasts. The crafted skin is of a nature we are not familiar with, and the drawings upon it no one has been able to decipher," the robed elder continued, "what the high council has not shared with you in the past is that these incidents have actually been occurring for many cycles now, but in only a few remote villages, and on a much lesser scale." At this startling confession, a disturbing murmur arose from the crowd. The mountain leader finished adjusting the heavy stone blade to his arm and swung it around warily.

"In an awkward way, this handles much like a Shikar!" which was a sword attached to the hand and forearm. He stated, examining its weight. He strode up to a pillar to test its strength, but the results were far from what he had expected. The glistening black blade carved into the stone as if it were raw flesh. A shower of sparks flew to the floor as a huge chunk of the decorative pillar fell at his feet. However, the ebony blade was left unscathed.

He stood back astounded as the men near him gasped.

The leaders of the mountain tribes concluded that these black stone items were designed for carving rock, though of a particular type of mineral that had never been seen before. Taking out his dagger, one of the men noticed that his steel-bladed knife could easily chip away at the dark stone itself …It was all very strange. Torg stepped forward and spoke up to address the crowd.

"While at the Cliffs of Chaos, we discovered a newly opened cave that connected to a hidden valley, where there was no sign of its existence before," he declared.

"Aye, we have observed many new cave systems among our old routes," another man added from the depths of the congregation. Again, the murmur of gossip grew louder at this revelation.

Torg picked up the curious skin with its erratic sketches and took it to the far wall were a set of torches blazed so he could get a better look at its painted designs. Holding it up against the light, he could see the hide was made of fine inter-fitting scales, like that of a large fish. The odd glyphs were opaque upon the smooth hide. Boggled, he folded it up and handed it to another clansman.

The man taking it, unfolded the pelt and cried aloud as he dropped the scaly parchment to the floor. Everyone was staring at the peculiar skin that lay in a heap on the tiled floor. The strange glyphs upon it now glowed like hot coals. He cautiously picked up the pelt with care, not wishing to burn himself but discovered no heat was coming from the writings as he cautiously passed his fingers across them.

"Clearly, whoever created these symbols meant them to be seen in the dead of night," he whispered in awe.

Chapter 4

The tribal alchemists performed various tests on the luminescent hide to discover its qualities. They had guessed that the strange glowing ink was created from some type of exotic plant, although its identity was still a mystery. The dark crystal blade and chisel were kept under tight lock and key for later presentation to the Evening season tribes when they arrived in Hagda later that cycle. In the city, several miners from various mountain clans eagerly offered goods the value of entire caravans for these unique artifacts, though without effect.

Torg returned to his camp and told the others of the news. It became obvious from much of the gossip which had spread throughout the city that not everyone had gotten the story straight. Before long, people were spreading wild tales of a black shikar that could cleave through mountains in a single stroke and magic symbols made of fire, and water beasts that could swim through the sky.

Tara eventually introduced Lela to his father, but the two adolescents spent much less time at his camp than the Chief would have preferred. It was the boy's first time to Hagda, so perhaps exploring the streets on his own and a little adventure in love wouldn't be so bad. The boy might learn a few things to help him mature.

Tara and Lela continued their harmless mischief. He even spent some time at her camp and met her Uncle. He had learned that Lela's parents were killed in an avalanche during a trek through the mountains some time ago. Lela's uncle was her only family now, he didn't pay much attention to the girl, but cared for her the best he could. Their clan was larger than most, and her presence was not missed while she and Tara combed the city. Many of the tribes chose to stay within the safety of the walls, and there was ample land beyond the gates for cultivating food crops and grazing their herds.

There were no taxes of any sort, but it was each tribe's responsibility to preserve the cleanliness of their camp areas and share in the burden of maintaining the buildings and water wells. Several men left on short treks to hunt for wild game far beyond the high city walls. Understandably, there were many who preferred the city life, and others who simply hated it entirely.

For a boy Tara's age, it was purely wonderful! He played with the other youths of his camp when he couldn't be with Lela. Sometimes their curiosity took them through narrow passages to the catacombs beneath the busy streets. There they found several locked doors and many more that were permanently sealed over. They snuck off with a few lamps so they could light their way.

It was uncommon for boys of his age to be underground due to the communal superstitions and fear of the shadows. Tara wondered how the mountain tribesmen could endure such spooky surroundings when they delved into deep subterranean mines to collect gemstones and metal ores, for in the darkness, the boys would jump and squeal every time they heard an unfamiliar sound. There were countless tales of spirits that lived in the shadows, thus, their adventures underground were exciting but always short-lived.

Tara took Lela back to the tunnels where he and his friends had explored earlier, and attempted to childishly but playfully frighten her. However, she was not amused; in fact, the ploy backfired when she proceeded to drag him even deeper into the dark winding labyrinths.

"If we're lucky, we'll find the graves," she whispered.

"Hold on now," Tara pulled away from her grasp, "I didn't agree to visit any tombs," he noted sternly.

"And I didn't agree to come here in the first place," she snapped back, "tricking me to come with you and trying to scare me and all. I thought maybe…"

"Maybe what?" he questioned innocently, completely boggled at her response.

"Well, I thought maybe you wanted to be alone with me, you know…" she teased while batting her eyes and rubbing shoulders with the confused boy.

He barely caught her wink in the dim light. Lela then caught him off guard by suddenly kissing him on the lips. Luckily it was dark and she couldn't see him blush. He felt a little giddy about that.

"Come on," she said, dragging him by his arm, "let's try to find those crypts."

Tara got completely lost at her lead and the oil in their lamp was running very low, but he wasn't about to leave her down here alone; besides, he wasn't all too sure about how to find his way back. He only hoped Lela did, with all of that stuff about 'female intuition' she had kept blabbing to him about all the time, while he wondered if it was some sort of mystical skill she had learned.

"Look over here," she whispered with excitement. Tara quickly made his way to her position. They stood before a gaping crack in the wall where several clay bricks and loose mortar had fallen away. To his astonishment, she began to desperately claw away at the brickwork in a most unladylike fashion.

The air within was cold and musty; they just barely

managed to crawl through the narrow crevice she had cleared through the broken plaster. This new tunnel was far gloomier than the corridors they had left behind and an eerie feeling prickled up Tara's spine.

"Don't be afraid, dummy," she giggled.

"I wish you would stop calling me that," Tara grumbled back with a curled lip. She gave him a quick peck on the cheek and grabbed his arm again, to encourage him to follow. It's amazing, he thought, what a woman could get away with on just a kiss. The tunnels in the crypts were crudely dug. There were several sets of shelves carved into every wall. Each nook held a body wrapped in burial cloth, many with bones poking through their rotted shrouds.

"Well this is real pleasant, Lela, can we go now?" Tara spat, coughing from the dust. Ugh, 'cadaver dust' he thought to himself while turning a disgusted frown.

"Not yet," she answered while they cut around another dark corner.

"What are you looking for?" he tried to whisper quietly as he ran after her, fearing he would wake the dead.

"These are the graves of commoners, but the Elders tombs are much more elaborate. My Uncle told me they are buried in vaults along with piles of gold and jewelry."

"And what," Tara stumbled, "...you are going to rob the dead?" the disdain in his voice was evident.

"They're already deceased, and they certainly don't need it anymore," she answered innocently, while flashing him an mischievous glance and a thin smile. Tara didn't quite approve but he was curious to see an Elder's tomb. Their oil lamp was getting awfully low, and Tara was afraid they would soon be hopelessly lost in the darkness of these catacombs and become one of its many permanent residents. As he shuffled down the dusty passageway, he fancied picking out an empty nook for himself.

"Look here!" She whispered excitedly while pointing ahead of them. Before them was a massive wooden door clasped with metal bindings, flaunting a pair of ugly gargoyles at either side. Oddly, the double doors shared a single solid brass ring. A strange sort of lock, they thought. She began examining the gargoyles in detail.

"Now what?" Tara inquired, not having a clue as to what she was doing.

"I'm looking for a keyhole or latch," she snapped back.

"A what?" Tara quizzed, completely boggled by her statement.

"A member of my tribe constructs trapped treasure chests, hidden locks, and secret doors," she responded, continuing her acute search.

"Why would anybody need such things?" Tara asked while helping her search the alcove.

"Much of the time mountain clans hide their heavy mining tools in such places like this, so we don't have to haul them on our pack animals wherever we go. We also create great storage vaults of wine that we stash underground so they may properly age, and we collect them the following cycle before taking them to market. The older the wine is, the more its worth!"

'You're saying the older something is, the more valuable it will be?' 'How entirely stupid,' Tara thought to himself.

"So you can see why we would need hidden locks and secret doors, lest some other clan or passing bandits might stumble across our stashes and take advantage of all our hard work," the girl confessed.

Tara reluctantly agreed she had a point as she deftly maneuvered her hands. To his surprise, part of the gargoyles claw twisted away as Lela handled it. The circlet binding the doors slowly turned, leaving the ring to fall to one side and the other panel free to open. Tara was amazed at the ingenuity of the lock.

He helped Lela open the door as dust and webs drifted lazily to the floor. Tara's overactive imagination had dreamt up the expectation of a large chamber lined with walls of gold and heaps of rubies and colorful gemstones scattered across the floor. To his disappointment, they were met with only a small and dusty room with a large stone slab lying upon the floor.

"This is called a sarcophagus," she stated eagerly, "we must remove the lid."

"There's no way we can budge this," he returned flatly, seeing how heavy it was.

Regardless, Lela heaved and grunted, getting her robes and delicate veils dirty as she crouched upon the floor. Tara began to wonder to himself, if all the mountain clan women acted this way? The slab moved a crack, then a little more. They both jumped to their feet when they heard the elated speech of numerous men behind them as their faint voices echoed through the distant halls.

"I think there are a few guards coming to haul us away," Tara cautioned, peering out of the slit of the doorway.

"They won't just take us away to be scolded by our clan elders," Lela warned, "most likely they will cut off our thieving hands as an example to others!" she mentioned hastily, suddenly grabbing Tara's wrist and bolting out of the tomb.

The deep voices of the guards were advancing and they could see a distant glow of torchlight approaching down the tunnel towards them. The children raced away as fast as they could without letting the wind blow out the flickering wick of their lamp. There was a new rousing of voices when they reached the open tomb they left far behind, and the sound of many feet in pursuit echoed down the halls of the labyrinth. Without pause, Lela led them through an exit back into the sewer tunnels. Tara felt a lump in his throat when the light of their lamp died out, the last drop of oil having burned away.

Lela only gave a quiet squeal of excitement, and she guided him down the narrow corridors as he felt her soft veils slapping upon his face in the darkness. Luckily the tunnels under the streets were pockmarked with thin shafts of daylight; some more diffused than others, although barely enough to see by.

She stopped again at the tunnel entrance, nervously looking for any sign of the city guards. They swiftly dusted each other off before slipping back into the mulling crowd above, trying not to look too conspicuous. They ran through the narrow streets of the marketplace and plopped down in the middle of a giant rug display. The vendor paid them no attention since he was busy haggling prices with several customers at the time.

Lela laughed out loud, and Tara couldn't help doing so himself. The sunlight felt good against his face as he laid back into the rugs, breathless. Looking over at Lela, he saw how beautiful she was, and so full of life. As he shut his eyes he felt her grasp his hand. She too closed her eyes and they both drifted to sleep among the plush carpets and droning chatter of the marketplace.

Tara slowly awoke to Lela placing grapes between his lips. Looking around and suddenly noticed that he was lying next to a fountain in a quiet little shrine, which was certainly not the place where he had fallen asleep.

"Where am... how did I..." he stuttered in confusion.

"Quiet now and each your lunch," she scolded, "I asked a young forest warrior to carry you here, little man."

Tara felt slightly groggy at first, but then nervously recalled all the trouble they had made for themselves earlier. His eyes widened and the boy quickly glanced at his hands to make sure they were both attached.

"Are the city guards..." he inquired nervously, but Lela interrupted his line of thought to put his mind at ease.

"You worry too much, Tara," she gave a quiet giggle, "...besides, I don't think grave robbing fits your skillset," she mockingly held a finger to her chin, rolling her eyes upward as if in deep thought.

"Youuu..." Tara grabbed Lela and tickled her.

They laughed for a while and got smashed grapes all over themselves. Tara noticed she was now wearing and exquisite gold headband of delicate chains holding a central ruby of no small size.

"Where did you get that?" he asked, touching the bejeweled headpiece which glinted in the light.

"Oh, here or there," she replied with a wry grin.

"Hmm, borrowing this are we?" he chastised her hobby of petty larceny with a stern glare.

"No!" She responded, pushing his hand away, "This is mine, I bought it a short while ago ...and I also got you a gift to."

"Bought? That's certainly not like you, Lela ...um, *what* gift?" Tara began to scold her, but was caught by a pinch of his own curiosity.

"Well I thought you were being so brave before," she said, buttering him up, "and for putting up with me in the dark crypts," she mentioned while lifting up a length of a twisted cloth from her side, "...that I wanted to get you something special," she said, while suddenly grabbing the knife from Tara's belt before he could react, "I will trade your old knife for this," she bartered, unsheathing an exquisite silvery shikar from the folds of silk. It was flawlessly crafted; he accepted it with grace and gently caressed the weapon with admiration.

"How could you afford this?" for metal weapons of such quality were expensive, if not rare.

"Oh don't worry, I got a good deal. I traded the brooch and a few necklaces for these," Pointing to her ruby headdress and the shining sword.

"What brooch?" The boy inquired with a dumbfounded expression washing across his face.

"The one I got from the tomb, dummy," Lela answered. He only gave her that look again, wishing she would stop utilizing that particular pet name.

"But there was no treasure, we never even got the lid open," he flashed back.

"Oh, we did, just a crack. I reached in before we ran out the door. I can only imagine what priceless treasures we had left behind," she stated dreamily as her eyes trailed off in wonder.

"You really shouldn't have..." he began to scold.

"Look here, Tara," she responded with a serious note, "I believe in living life to the fullest, and if some old fart died only to have all of his valuables buried with him, instead of giving them to his own family or tribe to help improve their lives, then I'm glad I disturbed his grave. People like that are selfish! What good is all that treasure doing anyone, buried and locked away in some dark and musty tomb?"

Tara couldn't counter her scorching response, and he certainly felt put in his place. After a few awkward moments, Lela's angry expression slowly melted away.

"Um, thank you for the sword, Lela," he finally answered to her fury with a humble kiss upon her cheek. She pulled away in apparent disdain, then suddenly gave a girlish giggle and kissed him back.

Tara wrapped his sword in a leather bundle and kept it hidden for the most part, for he didn't know how to explain his ownership of such an expensive weapon, considering the blade alone, was probably worth the value of his father's entire caravan.

Besides, it would be a grand mistake to tell anyone the story of his presence in the tombs, when doing so might likely lead to him losing a hand or two. Tara rubbed his wrists whenever that unpleasant thought crossed his mind. Tara's clan planned to stay for many more bands, but Lela eventually informed him that her own tribe might be moving on shortly.

"You're leaving? But you can't just..." Tara began to whine in a sad tone.

"I'm sorry Tara," Lela replied with anguish in her eyes, "but this whole incident with these mysterious items that were discovered by the elders and the numerous villages that were destroyed, has gotten the clan chiefs nervous."

"So what do we do? I don't want to lose you, Lela," Tara offered with a shade of sadness in his eyes.

She looked at him gently and put her hand to his cheek, "You're so sweet," she softly whispered with a tear running down her face.

"I know! You could join my clan ...well, I mean, if you would like to," Tara suggested with a measure of hope.

"I can't do that, Tara, and what would my uncle do without me? Besides, I don't think I could become accustomed to the way you rugged plainsmen live. Let's just enjoy the time we have left together," Lela offered as a condolence. Tara looked away, but she pulled his face back towards her, "I would like to sleep with you before we part," she breathed gently into his ear with a smile. Although, the ignorant boy was a little confused as to what the gypsy girl had meant by her offer.

There were countless festivals near the various shrines and town squares scattered across the sprawling city. Lela dragged him off to nearly every one of them. They saw stilt walkers, dancing troupes, and dramatic plays, and even daring fire jugglers who could breathe flames. There were many fabulous carnivals with entertaining shows. The most amazing were those with the limber acrobats, exotic animal tricks, and agile knife throwers as they performed seemingly impossible feats. Their skills of balance and strength were astonishing.

Lela wore her cat mask and got a similar one for Tara, which he was a tad hesitant to wear until she got a few cups of wine in him. Along a lone alley they stumbled across a hidden tavern but despite its run-down appearance on the exterior, the place itself was lavishly decorated within. Among the crowd, they found a large group of forest giants playing a game of shells and knucklebones in one of the carpeted lounges. There were fine meats and fruits, and here the spiced wine was flowing freely.

Many of the men huddled in their circles, laughed and groaned according to their luck at the dice. An ordinary man was brave indeed to gamble with warriors of their size, especially ones so drunk. They hit each other playfully with lively blows that would have crushed an ordinary man. Tara watched over their shoulders while standing upon his tiptoes, which was hard to accomplish even while the giant warriors were sitting. Lela sat him down and rubbed his shoulders while Tara appreciated her affections, and noted that he rarely saw a woman who ever matched her exotic looks. He felt very lucky to be with her ...and a little spoiled.

"There's something I want to do for you," Tara stated suddenly to Lela with a drunken smile flashing across his face. She just smiled back, not quite knowing what he had in mind. The boy got up and walked over to the giants playing dice, shouldered his way into their midst, then promptly unsheathed his silver shikar and placed it in the pile of loot before them.

"I'll wager this for a few throws," he boldly voiced to the forest men who were nearly three times his size.

The green warriors looked in astonishment at the small boy, then down at the exquisite sword in the pile, and then laughed so hard they spilled their wine.

"Of course, little bug," they roared. In his present mood, Tara didn't mind this new nickname, for it was certainly better than 'dummy' by any means.

He flashed an intoxicated smile towards Lela, who for some reason, looked quite worried at this turn of events. He seemed to notice for a moment, that wine dulls one's troubles. Perhaps Lela just needed a few more drinks, he thought to himself.

The warriors gave him several markers of value in collateral for his exquisite sword to use for play. Tara had his eyes on a few bracelets and coined belts that he intended to win for his lady, for he knew she was fond of such shiny baubles. He rolled the dice, for the game of knucklebones was a simple one. After accepting the bid, the players would roll their etched ivory die. The player with the highest score in one roll wins the pot. Any ties are re-matched again and repeated until there is one winner left to claim the spoils.

Tara lost this role. He scowled at their laughter, but he had many markers left. He recognized the gray-bearded chieftain he saw earlier among the crowd of players. Lela came up to him from behind to whisper in his ear.

"I admire your change of attitude and appreciate what you're trying to do for me, Tara, but..." she bent down closer, "these men don't like to lose, so there is no reason in playing," she cautioned him.

"What a pretty little flower...*burp*" one of the husky giants wheezed drunkenly, groping with a massive hand towards Lela. Before Tara could think of what he was doing, he slapped the giant's hand away with all his strength and then widened his eyes, as did Lela, in disbelief at what he had just done.

The giant stared at him for a confused second with a dumbfounded expression crossing his drunken face, but only managed to burst out laughing with the others.

"It seems..." he roared again, looking around to his companions, "that our little bug can sting!"

Clearly, the giants took the assault playfully as they did amongst each other. There was, of course, no way the small boy could possibly hurt the giant. They continued to play, each mumbling hasty prayers to their Gods for luck before each roll. Tara was holding his own, and everyone feasted and drank heavily until they were almost bursting. Then arrived a new member into the group of gamblers who began raising the wagers dramatically. He was an overly dressed man sporting a fine turban and embossed silks, and he held an arrogant look etched upon his lean face.

"Twelve chips," the rich merchant challenged, knowing that few at the table had so many markers.

"Bah, your gizzards are made of stone!" One of the giants snorted. The pompous merchant kept his smug posture, peering at the giant with his beady little eyes.

"Fourteen," the armored gray-bearded Chieftain retorted back in challenge.

"Sixteen," The merchant spat back again.

"Twenty," Tara shouted while throwing a large stack of his brass counters into the pile, feeling completely in the rush of the moment.

All of the men turned to stare at him in disbelief; the Merchant's face beheld the most surprise and was starting to turn an angry red. The rest of the giants only laughed, as they were all very amused at their little bug.

"Done," snapped the merchant while slapping down the majority of his markers, not looking very refined at all.

A few of the other giants added their markers together to meet the wager, then a few others, and more still from the crowd behind who didn't want to pass up such an opportunity to win such riches. There was an excited murmur about the room as the stack of polished markers raised ever higher, one atop the other, into a glittering pile. There where now well over a hundred chips at the center of the rug, more than enough riches to buy several tribes and live a life of ease for cycles to come. The bars rang as the markers were tossed together.

Lela, smelling trouble, grabbed their things and moved to stand close behind Tara while spreading her veils protectively about him as the dice were rolled. Each player had a different colored pair of carved bones to throw, so as not to confuse the tally. Everyone held their breath. Tara and a pair of the giants and the merchant were tied, the other losers all groaned in unison.

The crowd pressed in. A second roll, Unbelievable!

Astonishment flowed through the crowd as they counted three more ties. Another giant was out, and a third roll was called for. The men eyed each other suspiciously as they slowly sipped their wine, attempting to quell the bitter taste of desperation.

Tara felt a wave of heat flash through his head, this tension was making him a little dizzy. Of everyone there, he had the least to lose; merely a sword he had gotten for free. But still, it was a gift from his love, and of no small value itself, especially to him. The merchant spoke, addressing the final players.

"I see the boy has four more markers, perhaps we should sweeten the pot," the greedy merchant offered as he threw in the last of his markers.

The gray-bearded Chieftain borrowed four more bars from his clansmen and slammed down his chips; growling at the cocky little merchant as he did so. Tara could only comply, and was starting to feel a little sick to his stomach.

Time seemed to stop as the last of the dice ceased to spin and finally came to rest. Tara got an 8, the giant turned an 11, the merchant a 12. Everyone stared at the bones for a hushed moment to make sure that the count was right. But before anyone could react, the giant hit the small merchant square in the face. Tara thought for certain the man would have died from the blow.

Several women screamed as drunken giants roared, the merchants' personal bodyguards reacted, even if a tad too late, but they still fought the aggressors as a raging brawl broke out. Lela fell forward over Tara who looked around in confusion as the room erupted into flying brass markers, fists, and food. Something in sheer green veils with soft hands grabbed him by the arm, and flew him out the doorway and into the alleyway beyond.

There was a commotion in the streets as a fire suddenly erupted from a fallen brazier full of hot coals. Shouts could be heard echoing from down every street in all directions. Men and giants alike came running, while merchants and onlookers went scurrying out of their way. Lela threw Tara into an oversized vase poised beside a wagon. Drunk as he was, he landed awkwardly. She jumped in after him, covering the top.

"Ouch, my head," Tara complained as she quickly placed her hand over his mouth to hush him. Mingled shouts and screams of men, women, giants, and city guards could be heard outside of their clay container.

Unbeknownst to Tara, all forms of gambling were forbidden within the city, and Lela did not care to be remotely associated with their fellow players. For she had noticed among the loot of the ante, the unique brooch she had recently stolen from the tombs. When the officials discovered it was from the forbidden crypts, hands were sure to fly from their familiar wrists.

Tara quietly slid off into dreamland from downing far too much wine into his little body. Lela snuggled up next to him; the large vase was nearly empty, so they had plenty of room. She cuddled him as they lay upon a shallow bed of soft grain.

"Well," she groaned in mild disappointment with a shrug of her shoulders "...I did say I wanted to sleep with you," Lela sighed with a pout as she lay beside him, and she closed her eyes to join him in his dreams.

Chapter 5

Still a bit dreary, Tara was being shaken awake by his companion, but even after Lela let go of his arm he found it awkward that he was still rocking.

"We're moving!" she jostled him in alarm. It felt as if they were on a cart rolling along at a decent pace. Tara tried to stand up, only to fall back into the loose bed of grain from the lack of footing. They both helped each other up, bracing themselves as they lifted the tarp above them cautiously.

"Oh no!" Lela cried softly.

They were in the back of a huge wagon filled with similar vases as the one they were occupying. They were no longer in the city but at the rear end in a caravan of a forest tribe. The giants could be seen in the front riding mighty rorns. Tara looked behind them through the clouds of dust settling behind them to find that the tall towers of Hagda were nowhere in sight.

"This can't be good," Tara grumbled, slumping back into the soft grain beside Lela as they mulled their precarious situation, while sharing a deploring look of anguish upon their faces.

* * *

"For the fifth time... no! I have not seen your son!" Dooroo hissed at their tribal chief through his missing teeth. Torg turned away in anguish, perhaps his boy had just ran off with that new girl of his for a short spell, he thought to himself with measured concern.

The old man immediately felt ashamed for barking at Torg. He was an elder and an ex-chief himself, but Torg

was the leader of their clan and was only concerned for
the welfare of his only son. Dooroo, himself, detested
city life and wanted nothing more than to get back upon
the plains and under the open sky. He preferred the fresh
air of the prairies and the feel of the gentle winds, not all
of this unending noise and ruckus of the city he was
forced to endure. He was beginning to wish he could go
mercifully deaf, instead of toothless.

The tribal leaders were requested to keep records of any
suspicious activity, newly discovered caves, or any other
strange accounts they may come across. This task was
difficult enough since no one was educated in any form
of a written language in their society. Only a few
individuals, such as elders and their chiefs, were taught
how to paint vague images upon murals and the correct
designs for their pictographs. Many just scrawled crude
images of what they were trying to convey but
unfortunately, a majority of the time the commonly used
symbols were neglected and the renderings were at the
sheer whim of the artist who painted them.

Tara had been missing for several beads now and his
father even went to Lela's camp to inquire about his boy,
but the young girl's kin were only at a loss as to their
whereabouts.

"That girl always gets herself into trouble. Always
running off she is; and for the mercy of me, I can't seem
to keep her in one spot. Ever since she was a little girl
she's been untamable," her Uncle lectured, showing little
remorse, "but I will try to keep a lookout for your boy,"
he promised Tara's father.

Torg did not find much confidence in the old mountain
clansman, since his tribe would be parting Hagda in just
a few beads time. On his arrival back to camp, a worried

Dayrn came running up to him.

"I've heard from some of the other kids that Tara was seen gambling with the forest giants," the boy wheezed.

"How long ago?" the Chieftain demanded.

"A bead or two I believe, although I really didn't ask." Dayrn declared.

"Well, boy, where were they?" Torg inquired with elation at this news.

"There's a square near the northern towers in a building with a red canopy over the door. There was a huge fire, and a lot of people were arrested by the city guards and thrown into the pit!" the boy managed to get out in one breath while Torg mumbled to himself with worry.

The 'pit' was a fair-sized sunken courtyard that many large cities had built within their foundations. A cool dungeon cell would almost be pampering to drunkards and other rabble, so the officials punish such miscreants and other lowlife rogues, whose crimes weren't too serious, by placing them in a large enclosure and left them exposed out in the open sun without any form of shade, and they usually had to go without food and were given precious little water. This courtyard trench was built with high walls and placed below street level so that any citizen passing by could gaze down upon them. Occasionally, they were called spiteful names and splattered with rotten fruit if they weren't paying attention. A few beads under this humiliating treatment, plus time under the equally unforgiving and blistering sun, usually taught the poor embarrassed louts their lesson.

Torg combed the area for signs of his son, but Tara was nowhere to be seen among the miserable rabble baking in the pit. Unfortunately, the guards had no news of the boy, but gave him the location of the merchant who was assaulted, who might provide more useful information. With haste, the worried Chief made his way to the merchant's dwelling in the upper districts of the city.

A thickly muscled man with dark bronze skin stood guard at the entrance of the merchants abode, not with a tanned skin as would be expected, but his whole body was actually painted with metallic leaf. Tattooed upon the guard's forehead was the symbol of a protector and beyond his post a spiral of white stone steps disappeared behind the decorated garden walls.   Torg noticed the glinting sharpness of his spear and the row of daggers tucked within his leather belt.

"Who goes there?" he voiced boldly, as the sentry hailed him to halt.

"Torg, Chief of the eastern plains clan, I've come to see the merchant, Padra."

"Master Padra is very ill, and cannot see anyone," the guard replied coolly.

"I came to inquire about my son. He has been missing for several beads now, and the city guard told me to inquire here," Torg pleaded.

"Why so?" the guard inquired suspiciously.

"There was an incident at the gambling tavern, and I was told my son was last seen there," Torg stated.

The hulking sentry grunted to himself, "A boy, perhaps a cycle old, wearing a white and brown tunic?" the guard inquired.

"Yes," Torg asked trying not to sound elated, "have you seen him?"

"Hmm …another guard and I accompanied my master two beads ago to collect fees from his stalls in the south market. Master Padra heard of a game in a local bar;

your boy was there with a young lady in the company of those filthy forest giants. There was a scuffle in the tavern, and I have not seen the boy since," the guard admitted with a measure of regret.

This was troubling, for Torg knew that forest tribes were all too frequently engaged in exploiting unfortunate businessmen and fellow gamblers who could not pay their debts by chartering them as slaves, willingly or not.

"What happened after the fight?" the chieftain inquired.

"A fire broke out and many in the crowd fled. My master and a few of the forest giants were arrested by the city guards. The officials had discovered there were items among the booty that had been recently stolen from the sacred burial vaults. None but my master, Padra, could pay the exorbitant fines, so the other patrons were thrown into the pit. However, I heard the forest warriors were cleared of any offenses concerning the stolen goods, because their sheer size alone kept them from entering the local catacombs and robbing the graves. However, since they could not pay the fines for their illegal gambling, they were exiled from the city for this cycle," the bronze guard finished.

Torg returned to the pit to verify this with the city guards, who told him that the forest tribe he inquired about had already departed out of the southern gate less than two beads ago. The worried father was advised that he could identify the forest tribe by the icon of four diamonds upon their clan crest.

Torg and a fellow clansman packed immediately, they secured a couple of their strongest mounts and took to the trail in pursuit. Two beads advance weren't bad odds and they had a chance of catching them soon if they hurried, since two lone travelers could outpace a caravan.

However, Dooroo didn't appreciate taking responsibility of the tribe in their Chiefs absence.

"Come back soon, you hear! I'm too old for this!" the old man growled in disdain; although he humbly wished his clan chief a safe journey under his breath while trying desperately not to lose his composure.

The tracks of the giant forest rorns were easy to spot. Torg was certain that his son had gotten himself into a situation far over his stubborn little head, and had been taken into slave service to pay some form of debt. He would trade whatever he could to buy him off, though he couldn't imagine what Tara could possibly have had of any value to gamble with in the first place, while he began the long trek in pursuit of his lost son.

* * *

"The caravan has already reached the mountains," Lela flashed to her companion as they had both been debating about their unfortunate situation.

"I'm sure we haven't been asleep that long, we just have to follow the trail back to the gates of the city," Tara argued.

"Travel on foot, are you crazy?" she cried, "You've got boots on but I'm only wearing sandals, and our feet would wear to nubs before we could get within sight of Hagda," she blurted aloud. Tara just grumbled in reply.

"I don't know why we just can't stick our little heads out and say; *'"Hi there, we're just a couple of stowaways on your caravan, we apologize, but if it's not terribly inconvenient, could you take us back to the city, please?'* I'm sure they would understand," he blurted innocently.

"*Ugh*, you're not a dummy, you're an idiot!" Lela blared, and Tara flashed her an annoyed look for calling him that name again, "It is far too early for the forest tribes to be leaving Hagda so soon. They would only be on the road because they were banished from the city."

"How would you know that?" Tara babbled.

"Because, dummy, of that fight they started," she continued, "...and because forest tribes do not grow grain," she said, patting the thin floor of seeds they were sitting in, "so I presume they were booted out of the citadel before they could have these containers filled, and my guess is that if you stick your little head out of this jar they might just snatch you up and bite it off while blaming the whole situation on us as they chew your skull into grit!" she finally finished.

Tara was beginning to get that sick feeling again as he dwelled on her chosen words. Lela just braced her hands on her hips the best way that she could in the confined jar, trying to look poised and continued to leer at him. Tara looked at her dolefully.

"I'm sorry I lost the sword you had given me," he mumbled pathetically in remorse.

"And you should be!" she chimed without dropping her stern tone. She kept her snide look and made a show of glaring back at him while she removed her outer veils. As she did so, Tara noticed a strange bulge of cloth located in the small of her back. Lela dug into the shallow bed of grain under their feet, and to Tara's astonishment, she pulled out his prized sword.

"How did you...?" Tara's words trailed off as he grasped the shiny shikar in disbelief.

"Oh, well, you were drunk, and everybody else was busy fighting, so I helped myself," she declared with a smile. She reached behind her back into a secret pocket and removed two heaping handfuls of jewelry. Tara was a little dumbfounded but was very happy to get his sword back, regardless. He took a moment to lift her veils and examine the secret pocket in the back of her dress.

"Can't see it when I have my veils on, can you?" She retorted playfully, "Mountain clans usually sew in large pockets like this on our trail clothes to store extra rations and tools, in case of emergencies."

What kind of emergencies Tara couldn't imagine, but Lela seemed happy to fill him in. Mountain clans traveled to higher elevations where most trails were extremely narrow. Sometimes the paths fell away and there were constant risks of avalanches. They faced bad weather or cave-ins when working in the mines, or any number of other mishaps could happen, so you had to be prepared to survive on your own if you ever got separated from your tribe. Tara could see he had a lot to learn from this saucy little girl.

They both agreed that they had to slip away from this caravan as soon as possible. Lela quietly crawled out of the giant pot against his wishes and snuck out into the bed of the cart. She returned a short time later with a few water skins and an armful of flatbread for them to eat.

"All the giants are up in front except for one riding in the back, though it appears that he's fast asleep," she mentioned as they both peeked out of the tarp, "they drank more wine than we did during the festival, so hopefully they'll rest longer too," she uttered. The two young companions gathered their things and slowly crept out of the vase. The large mount of the sleeping warrior eyed them curiously as they clambered out into the bed of the cart.

Tara had seen many rorns before, but few ever so big as these. The plains people used baraths as mounts, which were simple to ride. They had small heads, two muscular legs and a long thick tail that slithered across the ground. The animals were very strong and could easily carry heavy loads nearly twice their weight. They had a smooth trot, and with a covered basket saddle strapped upon them, it was an easy feat to recline and catch some rest while astride one when traveling.

Rorns were ridden much the same, except their long legs made them taller and they were adequately built for speed. They were nimble climbers and could navigate over rocky terrain, but being finicky creatures, they only wore the bare essentials for a saddle and their gait was also fairly awkward. They had three large toes on each foot instead of the large fleshy hoof of a barath, and a very short tail that lifted high off the ground. The strangest sight about a rorn was that they appeared at first to have two heads; these in fact, were only their long eyestalks extending from their lean torso.

Lela gave Tara his cue, and they both jumped off the high wagon and rolled into the brush alongside the trail. Lela had timed it so that they would come to rest at the bottom of a dry stream bed. They held their breath while they watched the rear rider pass them by as they laid there in full view.

The giant was slumped over and snoring with a string of drool hanging from his chin. His mount kept one eye ahead to keep pace, while the other peered back at them in curiosity as the beast passed them by in silence and trotted ahead. After the wagons passed, they both let out a sigh of relief but kept themselves hidden for a few moments longer until the caravan disappeared from sight around the bend of the trail. Tara took off back down the road in the opposite direction at a leisurely pace.

"Where are you going, dummy?" Lela shouted behind

him. Tara stopped to turn around and stare at her with a
perplexed expression painted upon his face.

"Back to Hagda of course, what did you think?" he
replied sarcastically, completely astonished at her
senseless question but Lela just wrinkled her nose and
placed her hands firmly upon her hips as a signal that
another verbal lashing was forthcoming.

"That would be nice if we actually knew the path back,"
she snapped.

"What do you mean, there is only one trail here," the
boy stated impatiently as he pointed towards the road.

"There are countless trails that intersect along this way,
dummy, we would only manage to get ourselves lost,"
she responded in kind.

It was true that Tara didn't know how to follow trails
and wished he would have paid more attention when his
father had plotted maps. More importantly, he didn't
possess a device which all tribal chiefs carry, called a
Triad, which was a small pyramid-shaped device with
four levels. There is a hole in the top and a curved lens
in the second level down, and another with pinhole
patterns in the third. The bottom was then adjusted to
align with the patterns to the sunlight that came through
the lens; this told you which of the four directions you
were facing, and also what seasonal zone you were
currently in to navigate by.

Tara finally gave in. He didn't have a clue which
direction Hagda was, adding to the fact that giant rorns
traveled at a much faster pace, and had to finally admit
that they were likely much farther from the city than he
had first thought. Lela suggested heading towards the
high mountains that broke the horizon. She claimed this
would give them a better view of the land, and claimed

such mountain trails were usually well marked.

He grudgingly followed her lead. Besides, the mountains didn't seem too far off. Hopefully, she could get them out of this mess. Oh boy; was he going to get it from his father when they got back! The two companions quickly consumed their paltry supply of bread in no time at all and Lela tried to appear confident they could find a path; but after a while, he could tell that the harsh trail was wearing her out and her patience a little thin.

"We should stop and rest," Tara proposed after a long stint of following her lead, while realizing they were both neither dressed nor equipped for such an excursion.

Lela looked tired indeed; luckily the pair had escaped the giant's caravan before it reached the dense forests to the south. Tara could barely make out the edge of the plains that swept like a shallow bowl below them. This hiking uphill by foot was a chore, and to make it worse, the water skins that Lela had pinched were filled with wine rather than water, and drinking as they were to parch their thirst was beginning to make him feel a little lightheaded again.

Lela found a trail, but it was descending from the mountain in the opposite direction they wanted to go. Traveling cross-country without food supplies and in their city garb would be suicidal, and Tara began to long for his thick boots and traveling leathers. They followed the faint path upslope, anticipating that it would soon begin to descend. Hoping to get a better view, Lela went off trail to scout a little higher up the mountain. Tara stayed behind while she climbed the rocky cliff freehand, he wasn't about to attempt scaling cliff walls the way she did. It was a while before Lela finally came stumbling back down the hill.

"I found a fissure in the rocks, and since this trail is going nowhere, I think we should take a look. It could be a shortcut to the other side of this peak, where we would get a better view of the land below," she proposed. Tara wasn't in the mood to debate with her. If she wanted to play leader, so be it. Who was he to argue with a woman, anyhow?

The fissure she had discovered was many stories high and thinly split. It didn't seem too dark, so they dared to venture inside. The path was steep and littered with several thick boulders that impeded their progress. By this time they were beginning to feel the full effects of their wine and realized they had to find fresh water and something to fill their belly's soon.

The fissure continued to narrow, funneling into the mouth of a small cave. The grotto seemed short enough, as they could see a bare amount of light coming from the far side. There was no wood or brush nearby to fashion crude torches, but Tara was willing to brave the passage. There was a strong wind blowing out through the entrance, but it seemed to them that the current of air was unusually warm.

Lela appeared a little reluctant, but this was Tara's turn to take charge. Holding hands, they groped through the shadows to the other side and finally emerged onto a steep hillside of a large valley surrounded by sheer walls. It was much greener than anyplace either of them had ever seen before. There were huge trees that reached for the sky, and several flocks of birds skimmed the canopy.

The cracked ledges were precarious to tread upon, so they carefully clung to the rich vegetation growing on its face as they descended cautiously on the slippery rocks.

"This wasn't what we were looking for," Tara remarked with agitation.

"Have you ever seen such trees, Tara?" Lela exclaimed with bright eyes as she pointed towards the forest, "Look down there, a waterfall!"

Desperately thirsty at this point, the fresh flowing water was something worth investigating. They had several close calls as both of them slipped on the narrow path down the cliff side. The waterfall was huge but its stream bed was quite shallow, and within the clear blue waters they could see very tiny fish swimming near its banks. There were several species of plants and fruit trees here that they had never encountered before, but they were both hungry enough to try anything, so they nibbled on whatever looked edible.

Lela took off her clothes and washed them in the shallow pond by the stream, Tara only stared at her naked body in an awkward state of shock.

"What's the matter, you never seen a naked girl before?" she giggled, wrapping a huge leaf around her as she walked up to him. He was just planted to the spot, speechless. Tara didn't know if he should be embarrassed and began to mumble a reply. She only wrapped her arms around his neck and kissed him. Lela grabbed his hand and led him towards the pond.

"Come on, we both need a bath," she playfully giggled into his ear while she pulled off his dirty robes. In the memorable moments that followed, the seductive gypsy girl taught him a thing or two about women. After that experience, he just couldn't seem to wipe the smile off his face for a very long time.

They had stumbled upon a little paradise, but the boy wondered what nasty critters could be lurking among the thick foliage. This narrow valley was a veritable jungle; entire trees were covered in moss that hung like locks of woven hair. The soil was rich and green and there were numerous insects and birds he had never known existed.

"This valley is beautiful; I bet we're the first ones to ever find this place," Lela exclaimed in wonder.

Tara thought that she was probably correct but the fact was, paradise or not, they had to find their way back to the city. If they became trapped in this valley, they might live comfortably for several bands until the cold shadow of nightfall eventually enveloped the region, and they would freeze to death in the suffocating darkness.

"We really should search the far end of the valley for a way out," Tara suggested.

They both agreed it would be too dangerous to try to climb back out the way they had arrived. Tara quickly fashioned a spear with some strong wood and a sharpened stone. His shikar was deadly enough, but he wasn't about to fight at close range if they should happen to run across any large beasts.

He really just wanted something he could throw as he ran away. Tara, of course, felt he didn't need to explain the logic of his personal tactics to his lovely companion, lest his level of bravery be judged.

They made their way through the dense jungle, finding that the canopy of the trees was so tight that it nearly blocked out all the sunlight. The air was filled with high pitched whistles and the whooping of strange birds, along with the buzz of colorful insects. Tara was hoping one of those giant lizard creatures he had seen before didn't have a relative or two living here. The two youths suddenly stumbled across something quite odd.

"Well, I guess we're not the first ones here after all,"

Tara stated as he looked up the length of a huge totem. He had never seen carvings of this nature, and being the chieftain's son, he had seen his fair share.

The avian totem was carved of stone, a huge beast with a wide mouth holding a frozen expression in a freakish way that looked like both a grin and a snarl at once. Behind the bird-like statue, there was a small hut composed of enormous dried leaves settled next to the cliff wall. The shack was in complete shambles, but they were curious enough to investigate. Inside they found huge pots carved from wood, numerous baskets, and much debris scattered about the floor. Interestingly, the back of the hut opened up into a shallow cave that was covered from floor to ceiling in colorful hieroglyphs.

Lela suddenly screamed. When Tara jumped to her side, he saw she had uncovered the desiccated corpse of a man with black leathery skin and white tangles of hair.

"*Humph*, you'll blindly grope around in an old musty tomb but you jump at the sight of this?" Tara uttered with mild amusement.

"I just didn't expect to see a body," she mumbled back with a pout. Tara noticed that the poor individual seemed to have been dead for quite some time. Covering his body were numerous polka-dot tattoos arranged in decorative spirals. Lying among its feet were several pieces of broken pottery and worthless beadwork. Tara took a moment to cover its face with a scrap of ragged cloth; its blank hollow stare was giving him the creeps.

The symbols painted on the wall were what interested him the most, as there were lengthy depictions covering the entire interior of the small cave. He could tell from the drawings that there was a cavern some distance farther up the valley that held a tribe, but the likes of which he had never seen before. They were drawn in a funny way, with long arms and white eyes, and appeared to come from the belly of a demon out through the mouth of a cave. There was another tribe drawn in brown that fought with the ones in black. They used balls of fire to surround their village, one form could be seen rising upwards, but its significance was a mystery.

It was apparent from the pictographs that the tribes with long arms were far more numerous than that of the opposite clan that resided above. Curiously, the boy could not locate any drawings of what the tribesman hunted, such as large animals or prey, or even scenes of domestic life. However, there were several symbols that he couldn't make out, including one picture of what looked like a red egg with many holes on a stick that was repeated over and over with a ring of light around it.

"This indicates there's a village at the end of the valley, perhaps they could show us the way out," he offered while pointing at the illustrations.

"Well, we should try to find them, and tell someone they forgot to bury this old guy," she replied, motioning to the covered remains lying on the ground. Tara agreed and urged a measure of discretion.

"We should be cautious. From what these drawings say, they might not be too friendly."

Chapter 6

Back on the trail, Torg and his fellow companion were making good time and they estimated that the giants had just entered the edge of the vast forest, and were not too far ahead. His fellow clansman, Daig, had managed to track the huge prints of their rorns into the forest as their oversized cartwheels weren't hard to miss. As they approached the dense forest, a distant horn sounded and two mounted forest warriors came to meet them. Evidently, the forest clansmen had spotted them from afar long before they were even aware. The two giants approached the smaller plainsmen, who eyed them with a measure of distrust.

"Greetings, we come from Hagda. I am Torg, Chief of the Plains tribe," he stated while giving a cordial gesture of goodwill.

"Why do you follow us?" the giant man growled suspiciously while his comrade rode up beside him.

"We heard you had been banished from the city this cycle because your men were not able to pay the fines," Torg explained to the wary giant, who had rested his meaty hand upon the leather-wrapped club fastened to the side of his belt. Its blood-stained wood and long iron spikes hinted that it had seen much use in battle.

"And you would care to pay these dues for us?" the two giants jokingly inquired, "A few of our members were arrested and fined for their involvement in a common street brawl. Since all the valuables they gambled with were confiscated, they were forced to yield. We do not turn our backs on our clansmen, so our group departed together..." The large husky man added, "but still, you have not explained why you are trailing us?" he finished; leaning forward on his mighty rorn that towered over the two plainsmen.

"There was a small boy amongst the crowd at the tavern where the fight broke out. He is my son, and has gone missing since the incident with your clansmen. I came to see if he has been taken into ...uh, *service* for any debts he may have incurred," Torg conveyed while trying to practice a shade of diplomacy. The giant glanced over to his fellow clansman with a raised brow, then back toward the two small riders before him.

"Come, we will see about your kin," Upon that, they reined their huge mounts around and made haste back to their caravan. The plainsmen's mounts could hardly keep up with their guides as they delved deeper into the thick woodlands.

The forest clan's caravan was remarkably huge, not just in numbers but also in the sheer size of their wagons. The party rode up alongside a crudely constructed wood cage; inside was a man wearing a soiled turban and bright red pants. He jumped up at the sight of the two plainsmen, pressing his face up to the bars in desperation.

"Please, good sirs, if you will take me back to Hagda, I have a great uncle who is a very rich merchant, who will repay you twice over for my debts to these monsters..." he trailed off, looking directly at the scowling warriors who had overheard his slight. Their prisoner caught his breath and was quick to correct his choice of words, "...I mean, of these honorable tribesmen," he pleaded. However, Torg was paying little attention to the poor fellow as he eagerly inspected the dark cage for any sign of his son.

"Is there anyone else in there with you?" He asked, trying to see through the thick wooden bars. The poor fool within looked around and shrugged, relaying that there was not. In disappointment, Torg tried to block out the man's anguished pleas as he turned his attention back to the green warrior.

"He is not your son?" the giant inquired in a deep voice as he motioned his prisoner to back away from the bars.

"No, my son is only a cycle old. Are you holding anyone else?" Torg petitioned while trying to cling on to what little shreds of optimism he had left.

"No, no-one else," the forest giant confessed while shaking his head. Another giant of immense stature fell back to inquire as to their presence, he was a huge man adorned with a thick gray beard.

"I am Headsman Groheem, leader of this clan, who is it you seek?" he questioned loudly. His fellow clansmen shortly informed him of their venture.

"A boy in brown? Why yes, we have seen him. Our little bug with a silver stinger," he chuckled, although Torg was a little confused by this colorful description of his son.

"We are at a loss. From what we were told he was last seen during that tavern brawl where the fire broke out," Torg stated with hope draining from his voice. The giant looked around to address his men.

"Has anybody eaten a small boy lately, or perhaps tucked away one in his boot?" he shouted out loud, and a roar of hearty laughter erupted from his men in answer. After they quieted down, he again addressed Torg and his companion.

"As you can see, your boy is not in our company," he stated solemnly, "Perhaps he is still in the city..."

Interrupted just then, the deafening sound of a horn blasted twice from the head of the convoy while loud chatter arose from all around them. The forest chieftain hurled his mount around and made for the front of the caravan in haste. In a short moment, everything erupted into mass confusion. Daig gave Torg a terrified look.

"What is happening?" he asked in alarm, but Torg could only guess.

The chatter surrounding them from the thick woods evolved into an erratic hooting. An arrow came flying from out of the trees, missing them both narrowly and struck deeply into the post of the cage. The little man inside reeled about in panic, dropped down face-first into the straw and covered himself promptly with a blanket, while mumbling hysterically to himself in fear.

"Bandits!" one of the giants warned. The caravan halted and streams of arrows came flying through the woods as the giant warriors charged ahead to defend the attack. Unfortunately, the amassed roadblock they formed ahead with toppled trees and brush was only a diversion for the rear assault. They were trapped!

Torg and his friend could clearly see that the giants were outnumbered, and now many were fighting on foot since their mounts had been killed by the assault of arrows. Their rorns were most likely the victims of poor marksmanship, for such huge beasts were exceedingly expensive and were among the most valuable prizes of such a raid. The two plainsmen quickly determined that they were on their own in this fray as a dozen bandits riding young rorns came swarming onto the convoy.

Torg had never witnessed a bandit attack before, and armed with only spears, he was sure that they could not hope to defend themselves for long. At the moment, the giant Chief could not comprehend why his caravan was being attacked. One forest giant was equal to four men in combat, but his own comrades were being mercilessly cut down by the endless hail of arrows. The cowards would stay within the thick of the trees beyond reach as they picked off his warriors, one by one. He roared and caught one bandit off guard, who dropped his bow and tried to flee. Groheem threw a large spear that pinned the man to a tree, where a gurgle of blood fell from his lips.

Daig reined his barath around the giant cart and caught a bandit in the shoulder with his hunting spear. He unfastened his short javelins and began to mark his targets, but many missed in the thick brush. The rogue archers simply had a much greater range over them. Torg called to his companion to make their escape, assuming these brigands wanted the booty of the caravan and nothing else.

He turned just in time to notice a look of shock flash across Daig's face; an arrow had passed through the back of his basket saddle and into his side. The reins of his barath fell from his grip and to the ground. Torg slapped his mount forward and prodded Daig's mount lightly in the rear with his own javelin. The sharp jab caused the beast to fly forward, shrilling a painful whine. It burst through the underbrush, knocking two of the surprised marauders from their mounts. The basket saddle with Daig's limp body came undone and fell to the ground as it hit a low-lying branch, by chance, blocking two flying arrows that were meant for Torg.

He could hear the giant's shouts and bellowed war cries coming from the slaughter behind him, but there was nothing left for him to do but flee. Glancing behind, he could see that a pair of brigands had broken off from the

ambush and were tailing him closely, meaning to chase
him down. His barath was charging at full speed, but in
comparison to their rorns, his mount was having a hard
time with the brush and rocky terrain. Torg suddenly felt
a flashing pain pierce his back as one of the bastards had
made a lucky shot with an arrow.

Torg suddenly came upon the edge of a ravine but his
pace was too fast for his mount to halt. They both slid
down its steep side and it took all his strength tearing on
the reigns just to keep upright. Luckily, the creature's
heavy rear kept them from tumbling over. Both of the
raiders mounts faltered above them and refused to step
over the edge in pursuit. One of the bandits was
violently bucked off his mount as all of his arrows were
pitched to the ground as he landed square on his face.

Fortunately, Torg had put some distance between them
as he evaded capture, but he was sure they could easily
track him from the higher plateau. He continued his pace
along the river's edge while scrambling to keep well out
of range of their bows. He was exhausted and bleeding
terribly from his wound. Torg finally stopped to remove
the arrow from his back, but it broke off as he tried to
pull it out. A hot stream of pain surged through him and
he could not hold back the tears. He dismounted his
barath only to find the poor beast had also taken two
arrows from behind, both deeply lodged.

There was also a long jagged gash in its tail, and he had
failed to notice the creature's thin stream of blood that
trailed behind them. Torg could see that the animal was
mortally wounded and wouldn't last long.

He found an alcove beside a shallow stream. Making
sure they were well hidden, he unfastened the woven
saddle and left it in the brush. Shortly thereafter he

passed out, completely forgetting the habitual practice of slipping the bead ring on his belt to track the time before he fainted.

The bandits had expected an easy prize, for they had thought that a caravan coming from the city was bound to be overfilled with gear and supplies; but to their great disappointment, most of the cargo wagons and their crates were completely empty. They took out their anger for their losses on the destitute captive in the cage. He was tortured for a short time before being set free. His battered body did the best it could to run as they all stood behind him laughing, until the fleeing man saw an arrow, then another zip past him, until finally, one hit home in the square of his back.

The looters had lost more men than they would have expected during their ambush. Forest giants were a formidable foe in hand-to-hand combat but were slow and lumbering, and made easy targets for their archers at a safe distance. They took their bounty of the meager treasure at hand. They packed the empty grain pots and few rolls of furred skins, and then proceeded to carefully clear the trail of any evidence that a skirmish had ever occurred. The bodies of the giants were buried in shallow graves far from the main trail and covered with loose brush.

One of the rogues boasted of the giant chieftain he had killed with an arrow through the neck. He proudly brandished the former owner's enormous hand knife, which to him, was the size of a short sword. The bandit leader fashioned a loop for the weapon, woven from the victims' own long gray beard he had sliced from his severed head. A pair of his men reported that one fool riding a barath had escaped to the south, but he was of no concern to them; for it was just a lone plainsman who was ill-equipped for this country. They would be on their way soon, to hide amongst the dense forest and plan their next foray.

Torg awoke to the sorrowful whining of his mount, a long whistle-like sound echoing its pain. He was not feeling too well himself. Torg had removed the arrows from the baraths rump but could do nothing to suture the massive gash in its side. He could only try to make his way back to the trail and limp back to the city.

Desperately searching his supplies, he could not find his triad compass and was missing all of his maps of this southern realm; all of which must have fallen from his saddle as he had fled down the ravine. Luckily, most of his rations were not lost as well, during his mad dash out of the forest but what was left would only last a short while, regardless. He had no idea what type of game was available here to hunt or where to find edible food in this strange forest terrain.

With little choice, he followed the small river down the valley upon his injured mount. A Few times the lone plainsman thought he had spotted more of the raiders in the distance, so with discretion, he kept hidden and out of sight within the thick of the timber as best he could.

There were high mountains to either side of the valley with a dense forest snuggled in between, and a rocky riverbed running along its midway. He knew he was hopelessly lost, and the wound in his back throbbed terribly. Torg finally chose to climb the nearest mountain to a point where he could get his bearings.

He did not wish to travel through the forest again for fear of the outlaws, who he anticipated did not want to leave any witnesses alive to tell of the encounter, and he feared they were most assuredly tracking him down at this very moment. Food rations were starting to run short and his inured mount was noticeably weary. Torg considered himself lucky to have made it to the lowest rift of the gorge. He could see across the valley to the mountains on the other side and noticed something about them did not look quite right, as they were oddly bowled in its shape. He searched the distant horizon for signs of the city, but the haze of weather did not allow him to see across the basin.

With a spark of emotion in his weary eyes, he was glad that he had not found Tara with the giants. Now hoping, perhaps, the boy had just run off deep into the city with that distracting girl of his; but he would certainly get a firm scolding when he got back. Looking out across the landscape he could see there was a gentle slope to the valley beyond and a mass of clouds laid low where the air was moist. He did not find any worn paths, but at least the ground here was smooth enough for his wounded mount to traverse.

The wind was getting much stronger and he could see many birds ahead breaking the pattern of the sky. It was strange not to follow a trail, and the seasoned chieftain began to feel a curious kind of freedom. His mount eventually faltered and stumbled. The creature lay exhausted; Torg could see that the bleeding from it open wound had worsened. He stayed there a silent moment until the animal gave its last breath. He considered for an instant about taking some of its flesh as rations but he had nothing adequate to carry it with, and he didn't care much to smell like spoiled meat, which would likely only serve to attract local predators.

"The chief without a tribe," he laughed weakly towards

the open sky. Here he was in the middle of nowhere, in between the mountains and forests. He just couldn't imagine why anyone would want to live in such rugged terrain. 'Well, at least I'm not the chief of a snow tribe,' he thought to himself in a dazed moment as he recalled the stories he had heard of the bleak and icy tundra that reached across the southern territories.

His injury had only been getting worse; since the arrowhead had broken off inside his back while the bleeding continued to seep through the bandages. He tried to bind his wound tighter, but this only made it harder for him to breathe. If only he had been shot in the chest instead, at least then he could see what he was doing and attempt to remove the arrowhead. Torg began to wish he had just stayed in Hagda; then at least, poor Daig would still be alive. At this thought, he began to feel a gripping sense of remorse over his fallen friend.

Perhaps it was stupid of him to worry so much about Tara, and forego his formal responsibilities to the clan just to run off after his wayward son. Most likely the young lad was probably back with his tribe by now and playing with the other children of the clan. Tara was a strong boy and could take care of himself, and Torg realized that he was being far too overprotective of him.

His wound began to open and the pain became evermore severe from the rough hiking by foot, and Torg was beginning to feel a little dizzy as time drifted on. He was losing too much blood, and knew it. He began to notice a soft beating roar flowing towards him from the distance and the air began to smell of salt. He looked ahead as a thick fog drifted in patches around him as a wide ocean unfolded before his eyes.

It could only be the Sea of Wrath, as he remembered its

placement on his maps. He glanced at his belt loop in confusion; had he forgotten to keep count of the beads? How long had it been since the attack? Certainly, he could not have traveled this far, and all in the wrong direction. As he shook his head a feeble laugh escaped his lips, the seriousness of his dire situation somehow escaping him.

Torg stumbled on, reaching the shores and found solace in its cool lapping waves, oblivious to the danger; only thinking how strangely peaceful and serene it was as he stared out over the glistening waters. The ocean was so beautiful, and was an impressive sight that few migrating tribes would ever have the chance to see in their lifetimes. With the sunlight sparkling upon its waters and the surf beating steadily upon the shore, he found that the sound of the waves calmed his pain and soothed his slowing heartbeat.

Quite weakened, he collapsed onto the moist sand, squinting at the glare of the bright sun high above. There was a ring of glowing light around the blazing orb in the sky above, '*How very strange*,' he thought to himself, wondering why he had never noticed that phenomena before. Torg, chieftain of the plains tribe, felt exhaustion overcome him. He lay there listening to the gentle waves and the cries of the distant shorebirds.

Gazing into the sun, he thought ...no, he was sure now, that he could see the face of his beautiful wife in the glow of the bright sun, she was smiling at him. Torg no longer felt like he needed to cover his eyes in the burning light, for the sun didn't seem so bright anymore. His breath faded, while beneath him, a stream of red swirled in the shallow waves that softly caressed his face.

Chapter 7

As they walked along, Lela kicked off her sandals and ran ahead barefoot across the soft jungle floor. Tara could see that there was something strange about the distant cliffs but he couldn't exactly determine what it was. Lela paused as she turned to look back at him.

"What's the matter, Tara?" she gleamed.

As the sunlight washed over his face, Tara had a sudden feeling of sadness overwhelm him, but he didn't know why, and he tried to shake it off.

"Uh ...I, I don't know," he muttered with uncertainty as Lela just gazed at him with concern. "We should just be more careful, so don't go running off."

"If you keep acting so grumpy, people might start to think you're not getting any!" she giggled as she ran up to kiss him again, only to slowly pull away. She could sense something was terribly wrong; it wasn't like Tara to act this way.

Their pace was hampered and slow, for the jungle foliage was getting thicker as they progressed. Every so often they stumbled across a clearing or a short path that was obviously made by design, but for the most part this area had been reclaimed by the lush plants.

"I don't get it," Lela voiced, "we haven't come across anyone and yet it seems to me like these people you described have been everywhere in this valley."

"Well, they might only have a temporary settlement where those cave drawings implied," he suggested.

"Look!" She cried, jumping for a plump red fruit she noticed hovering high above their heads.

Lela tried unsuccessfully to reach the lowest of many enormous globes of fruit that hung in the forked branches of a glossy black tree. She even tried throwing a few rocks several times to break its stem, until she gave up and tried to climb it. She hiked up her veils and launched herself upon the lowest branch, where she promptly slipped off the limb and fell on her rump. Upon seeing this, Tara couldn't stop laughing.

"Hmmm, I don't think climbing trees fits your skillset," he blurted while mocking her as he rolled his eyes, in the same gesture she had done to him before. She only laid there frowning while gazing at her buttery arms.

"The trunk is slippery with a type of wax or something," Lela whined while staring down at her greasy hands.

Tara poked his spear at the fruit she had tried to grab, it fell to the ground and burst open into several chunks. Lela skipped over to try to taste its meat but promptly spat it out in disgust.

"Yuck, it tastes really gross," she belched while curling up her nose.

"Well, this one is softer and red, the ones higher up are yellow, it's probably just overripe," he suggested.

"Not that, I mean it tastes *weird*," she replied, still spitting and wiping her hands on the grass. Tara went up to the tree and noticed with a swipe of his finger that the skin of the smooth bark was covered in an oily substance. The stems of the fruit higher up were visibly longer and much thicker.

"Hey, look at this," Lela mentioned, picking through the decayed fruit that had previously fallen from the tree. She pried off the hardened outer skin and yanked out the giant seed within. It hung firmly on the end of its long and sturdy stem, its shell punctured through with many holes. Waving it about menacingly, she concluded it was a bit too light to use as a war club.

"Hey, this kind of looks like that picture in the cave!" she declared, and they wondered what it could mean. Obviously, he would have to get one of the ripened fruit from above if he was going to solve this puzzle. After many pitifully crude attempts at building a ladder, Tara finally gave up and simply tried his aim with the spear. After much grief of trial and error, Tara finally hit one seed that snapped and fell to the ground. This one was also equally inedible.

"Well so much for that," he grumbled.

Lela took out her knife and peeled off all the skin as the bright yellow pulp fell away. She took out her flint.

"I don't think it will taste any better cooked," he advised, "besides, all the wood around here is far too green to burn for us to make a proper fire," Tara professed. Lela ignored his input, but as she tapped her flint together, there was a sudden orange flare and they both jumped back in alarm.

Lela had ignited her flint onto the moist pulp of the seed, where it burst into flame and burned ferociously like a bundle of oil-soaked rags. The hungry flames started reaching higher and ever closer to the overhanging branches of the strange black tree. He could see the danger that was coming and quickly doused the fire with dirt, but the ripe seed continued to smolder despite his efforts.

"Looks like I found our firewood," she smiled.

"Or firefruit, you mean! I've never seen anything burn so fiercely. We could sell these in Hagda in place of torches and lamp oil," Tara exclaimed.

Lela cautiously took up the large seed by its stem and

held it aloft as the burning embers at her feet continued to fight their way through the damp soil. Lela played with her blazing toy, twirling it around like a fire dancer; although she was careful not to get too close to the oily black tree, lest the whole thing go up in a ball of flame.

They walked back down the shady jungle path; however, this time their way was brightly lit by Lela's firefruit torch while shadows danced beyond the foliage as she passed. Tara noted to keep his distance, since most of the time she would thoughtlessly swing it around a bit more playfully than he would have cared for. They nearly made it to the far end of the valley when Tara noticed something ahead through a gap in the trees. He tried to extinguish Lela's torch but to his frustration, was unsuccessful at the task. He finally hid the burning seed behind a large wet log where it smoldered in the moist soil as it continued to sizzle.

He scouted ahead and found the remnants of a large settlement, but not a soul was to be seen, so he made his way back to get Lela. Tara removed the silver shikar from his belt and entered the village with Lela trailing behind, hand in hand; and after retrieving her torch, she had to be careful not to get its flames too close to the huts that were composed of dried brittle leaves.

There had been a sizable community here at one time, but it appeared to have been abandoned long ago. From what he could tell, they may have never returned the following cycles of the sun to reuse this place. Tara never heard about a jungle tribe, thinking perhaps he had mistaken those for a valley clan.

"There is no one around," Lela whispered.

"This is a huge village and not beyond repair with a little effort, I wonder why this tribe never came back to use it during the daylight seasons?" Tara debated.

The village was snuggled near the end of the valley with towering cliff walls enclosed tightly around it. When they began to search the cliff face for another outlet, it was only then that they began to notice the strange details of their surroundings. The walls of the bluff were plastered with intricate carvings. It was truly fantastic, the entire cliff face was riddled with windows and balconies, and decorated with finely detailed etchings.

There were huge jungle vines crawling through the structure where a few of the invasive plants had begun to obscure the fine workmanship. It was obvious these carvings had been here for many ages. They both agreed they would most likely find an exit through one of the open doorways speckled around the cliff base. Several of the portals were placed at ground level but far more were positioned much higher, with no apparent way to reach them without a tall ladder.

Most of these tunnels were dark, though often shallow. Few of the rooms went far beyond the rock face, where conveniently placed windows were chiseled out to let the sunlight through. Inside, there were narrow stairways which sometimes led through large holes that had been cut into the ceilings to reach other rooms; however, most of these were inaccessible without some type of rope or ladder. Lela's firefruit torch continued to burn steadily for an impressive length of time. Eventually, the companions returned to the village courtyard while feeling a shade discouraged.

"I can't believe there's no way out," Lela sighed.

"Well, we haven't explored all the chambers," Tara charged, waving to the numerous darkened doorways around them that scarred the cliffside, "we should go back outside and try to find something to eat, and maybe gather a few more of those firefruits in case that thing burns out," he suggested while pointing at their flaring organic torch.

They made their way back to the black tree and collected a few of the combustible fruits, and scrounged for edible roots and berries they found along the path on their route back to the deserted village. Tara thought it strange that there were no signs of small rodents around, but then again, he assumed that any animal could easily hide behind this curtain of thick foliage. By good aim and sheer chance, with his spear, Tara wounded a large bird they had found. After chasing it around for a while, he managed to finish it off. They discovered a clay fireplace in the village that was still in reasonably fair condition, and eagerly cooked themselves a warm meal.

The two young lovers lost all sense of time as they enjoyed their little paradise, exploring the jungle, the caves ...and each other. As usual, Lela went searching for treasure, and considered it quite odd that there weren't any burial tombs or even grave sites to be found here.

"None that you could find, you mean," Tara remarked.

"Well you would think they would put them in these caves somewhere, but there aren't any signs of tombs that I could see," she spilled.

"Well some tribes burn their dead to ash in funeral pyres; and besides, you did find a few trinkets to keep," Tara added on a positive note.

"Nah, these are worthless," she sighed, looking at some discovered beadwork she held loosely in her hands. Most of the jewelry was cracked and broken because of its age, and she thought it odd that the former inhabitants had left them behind.

They used the firefruit pulp to cook their meals but meat was scarce, and the tiny fish in the nearby pond were far too small to consider. They tried to remember all the rooms they had already explored, and that's when Lela suggested that they use a few old seashells they had found to mark their way. They made a system of chalking symbols for any rooms or hallways they had already visited, and continued on their exploration. A few of the corridors ascended steeply, leading them several stories above the Jungle floor. Just as Tara looked out the window across the abandoned village and up the cliffs to the bright sky above, something caught his eye. He could have sworn he saw a form moving in one of the windows on the opposite cliff. Lela startled the boy as she approached him from behind.

"I think I found a passage that was purposely sealed off, Tara. They didn't brick it up like some of the others, but jammed the entire length of the hallway with dry wood and debris instead," she explained while Tara thought that was very strange indeed.

They went back to the blocked hallway to take another look. In the gloom, Lela pointed with her torch around the barrier of dead foliage.

"You can see through the cracks of debris that they piled it in here pretty thick, and it goes on for some ways. It would take forever to clear this out; you would think this was their garbage dump or something," she declared with a bewildered frown.

"Well, I don't know, but I'm not about to try and carry all this out of here by myself just to see what's on the other side," Tara stated flatly, "Let's keep looking."

As she turned to follow him, Lela caught her veil on one of the thorny twigs sticking out of the jumble of branches and she carelessly slipped and dropped the fireseed. Tara grabbed for it quickly but it was too late. In a frightful moment, the blockade of dried logs and leaves caught fire in a fury of dancing flames. Within moments, the heat became so unbearable inside the confined hallway that they had no choice but to flee for their lives.

Coughing in the dense smoke spouted from the corridor, Tara dragged Lela out of the dwelling alongside him. Columns of black smoke poured out of a few adjacent windows. They could only watch helplessly as the fire burned fiercely. It was a long, long while before the smoke died away and they could return to the passage.

In the meantime, Tara tried to investigate where he thought he had seen that shadow move in the distant window across the courtyard. Unfortunately, there was no way of telling which room it was, or even if the passages there would allow him to reach the higher levels. He finally shrugged and dismissed the sighting as possibly leaves blowing in the breeze; however, from that moment on he kept a wary eye on the upper windows.

The two adolescents spent much of their time playing in their lonely valley. Most of the birds were too quick for Tara's unwieldy spear, so he gave up hunting for meat and they survived on a diet of berries and leaves. After scouting the valley walls, he was beginning to believe that only creatures with wings could escape this valley.

Lela collected many varieties of delightfully colored flowers and placed a few in her braided hair. From time to time, Tara practiced with his small flute, the music from it echoed from the cliff walls, created an aura of an eerie peace colored with foreboding. They only ended up discovering that the rest of the carved chambers led absolutely nowhere, and were unable to locate a means to reach the rooms above. Eventually, the single corridor that was barred to them previously by the burning brush was the only one that was left unexplored.

The charred debris was almost fully consumed, all that was left was a few smoldering ashes that refused to die. They had both lost all sense of time and neither of them had bothered to keep track. Tara was sure he was being missed by now and wondered what kind of trouble he would be in, and Lela was certain that her tribe had moved on to the mountain trails without her.

They discovered that the burnt hallway was by far the deepest one yet, and had been laboriously packed with debris for hundreds of feet down its entire length. Certainly, burning it away had been the quickest way to clear it, even if it was a reckless accident. The walls were charred black and the smoke had left layers of thick foul soot clinging to the ceiling that swayed eerily in the warm breeze of escaping heat.

Unfortunately, the hallway descended farther below, rather than rising to the upper levels, as they had hoped it would. Beyond, were many empty rooms and sets of stairways that continued downward. Oddly, a few of these passages led to abrupt dead ends, but at the bottom of one long stairwell, they discovered a dark gaping hole set in the floor.

"It appears they breached upon a natural cavern here," Tara surmised as he peered warily over the edge.

"Seems so, but still, if they wanted to, they could have just bricked this over and still used the other rooms behind us, instead of going to the insane effort of blocking the entire corridor like that," Lela remarked.

"They probably thought the other rooms were unsafe because they might cave in without knowing how close they were to the cavity beneath them, I don't know, you're the mining expert here," he chuckled.

"Well, maybe. If this was just dirt, I might agree with you but this is bedrock they had dug through. I would expect they should have bricked this up a dozen feet from here or put up a warning instead of blocking the entire hall so far up the corridor," she aired while Tara agreed that the crude barricade didn't make much sense.

They both peered down into the blackness of the hole. For lack of finding a loose stone in the area, Tara lit an extra seed torch and dropped it into the open pit. It flickered on a light draft for a long moment while it fell, before bouncing off a few distant walls and disappeared out of sight. They looked at each other with wide eyes …it sure was a long fall. They both stepped back cautiously from the crumbling edge.

"Hold on, can you see that down there?" Tara noted.

"See what?" she asked. Tara moved their torch away behind her head to shield its glare from her eyes.

"Can you see *that*?" he inquired once more.

Lela could make it out now. Peering down into the hole, she could see faint patches of light that had not been there before. However, they were so far below them that she couldn't make out what they might be. They retreated through the gloomy hallways and back outside into the comforting sunlight.

"I don't see any other way out of here, how about we gather some vines and weave a rope, and find out where that cavern leads?" Tara inquired.

"I thought you were afraid of the dark! I almost had to drag you kicking and screaming through those catacombs under the city," she finished with a teasing giggle.

"Well that was with a tiny oil lamp, but these," he

assured her while holding up a raw firefruit, "...are far more useful.   Besides, we have already searched everywhere else," he concluded.

The pair agreed they had to find their way out of this valley and back to Hagda as soon as possible, lest their clans leave without them, and they wouldn't survive on their own without a way to travel across the land.

The young couple gathered fresh vines and braided what they considered to be a durable rope. They had to heave a large dead log from the jungle into the hall and all the way down the stairwell, bracing it the best they could over the pit so it would serve as an anchor for their rope, for the interior walls were quite smooth and there was simply nothing near the pit that they could possibly secure it too.

Tara suggested that only one of them should go down to investigate while the other stayed behind, debating that he was stronger and could make the climb back up much easier than she could. Lela argued that she knew far more about such caverns and underground mines, and she could hold her own besides. Personally, he didn't like to squabble, so they both concluded to make the drop into the cavern together.

Tara made triple sure that the anchoring log was secure and they began their descent into the frigid darkness below. They came across the patches of light, which turned out to be a type of mold that grew on the bare rock. As they moved lower, they noticed this same gray lichen above their position glowed much brighter after their passing. Lela said it was from their extended exposure to the torchlight but Tara had a hard time believing her, even with the proof right in front of him.

Strangely, the side of the cavern walls did not seem

completely natural. They soon found a countless number of rounded nooks that appeared scooped out of the rock, which made him guess that perhaps a few adventurous villagers had made their way down here before. Lela pointed out that the niches in the stone were on all sides of the shaft, and much too far apart to be used as steps. Tara shut his mouth for a while after that.

After descending nearly a hundred feet, they were beginning to run out of rope and had so far discovered nothing of interest. Luckily, the shaft itself began to level out gently so they could continue on by foot. Lela saw a faint light up ahead but it only turned out to be the torch they had dropped earlier into the pit, still burning brightly as it lay upon the stone floor. She went to retrieve it, even though it leaned precariously on the brink of another vertical chasm.

"Just forget it, we've got plenty more," Tara cautioned.

"I can reach it," she voiced stubbornly.

Tara could see the chute they occupied turned ahead and widened gently as it continued past the dark cavity. Lela slipped slightly on the slick flooring, startling him. He went to grab her arm as she bumped the torch she was trying to recover, and it slipped into the adjacent pit. Gripping onto the edge of the void, they watched as the fireseed fell, mesmerized as massive stalactites and cavern walls rippling with formations, flashed into momentary view.

Oddly, it wavered as though in a brisk wind while it fell for what seemed like hundreds of feet until it finally reached the bottom of the cavern. Though the most startling thing that caught their attention, was when the torch finally came to settle on the cavern floor far below. What appeared to be multitudes of little black insects scurried away to escape the burning torch, but it slowly dawned on the two youngsters that this was an illusion of the light. The combination of their height above the cavern floor and the dancing firelight had deceived their sense of perception.

In the bright flickering torchlight below, they could see those creatures beneath them were much larger than they had first appeared. A faint whisper of strange voices arose and scores of glowing eyes reflecting in the light, slowly turned upwards to stare back at them.

Chapter 8

Back at their camp in Hagda, Dooroo was getting increasingly edgy and impatient with the members of his clan. He considered himself far too old and senile to be acting as leader for a whole caravan, especially for a second term. He found himself stuck wasting his breath settling details of minor squabbles for his tribal members, while trying to exercise a fair measure of diplomacy. Honestly, he would much rather be spending his days solely paying attention to his aches and pains, rather than the needs of the whole tribe. Where had Chief Torg disappeared to, anyhow?

The acting Elder of the Plainsmen was beginning to get worried, for Torg and Daig had been gone for several more beads than expected. There were no more forest tribes residing in the city to inquire with, and as yet no one had seen Tara or his little mistress. The local council of the High Elders informed Dooroo that a public notice would be posted, but advised that they could not make any promises outside of that; for in their open society, it was common for people to be adopted by other tribes at will and they were not bound to any one clan. This setback made Dooroo even more irritable than his usual self. He could only wait another band before they would be obligated to elect another tribal Chieftan from one of his own clansmen, if Torg didn't show up, and soon!

The stories going around the city about the strange and mysterious artifacts were getting wilder by the moment. The elders could only try to enforce the facts. Even so, as time passed and rumors that spread these tales became even more exaggerated, to downright preposterous.

Surrounded by an audience at a central stage in the city, one of the high elders recited a legend that was rarely told. An era ago, there had been an ambitious venture to explore the dark side of their world. Contests were held in all the major cities to discover the bravest and the strongest of warriors who could endure this monumental and daring feat. For many seasons, arena games were posted where a series of competitions, combats, and personal duels were judged. All the clans and tribes participated and contributed towards this single goal, for everyone wondered what strange mysteries they would discover dwelling beyond the creeping veil of night that had forever chased their people across these lands.

There were great festivals and clan rivalries of the likes never before seen, as each tribe competed for the honor of being a part of this historic crusade. After much planning and preparation, a dozen men were finally selected to make permanent camp in the famed city of Silistra, where they would face the mystery of nightfall.

Many stories had been woven that only demons and the spirits of the dead walk on the dark side. They said it would become so cold that it would freeze the blood in your veins and turn you into a statue of flesh. They wove tales of deities and specters who fought fantastic battles to keep the sun balanced in the sky. It was truly a divine mystery despite the countless superstitions and ghostly folklore, but they were determined to solve this riddle.

Every tribe had allotted provisions to the chosen few for their long encampment to last through the season of nightfall. Those few brave men left behind by the last of the evening tribes bade them safe journey through the coming darkness, and continued their migration onward to chase the sinking sunset.

The brave group of heroes had the entire palace to themselves, along with massive storerooms stocked full of select provisions of food and wine during their lengthy encampment. All the doors and windows were fitted with thick skins and furred hides to protect against the dreaded cold of night. Their Shamans had taught them how to perform magical chants and prayers designed to shield them from unseen spirits. These champions were to make an account of their experiences through the dark season by keeping a record of paintings in the main hall, for the Elders wanted to know if it would be possible to survive the season of darkness.

As they continued their migration across the land, their people eagerly awaited the coming of dawn when they would once again reach the fabled city to learn of their fate, but upon the following cycle when the first morning tribes had arrived in Silistra, they discovered that their heroes had disappeared and not a single one was to be found. Their recorded murals did not explain the mystery of their absence, for no one could interpret what they truly meant.

The first paintings along the palace hallway suggested that the temperature dropped, as was expected. Then came gales of wind accompanied by harsh sandstorms. The murals showed that a band later, vast hordes of small bird-like creatures had flooded into the city. Their wings were much too short for flight and these pests would scour every nook and cranny of the city for food. The pictographs proceeded to reveal the men had to chase these scavengers out of their storage rooms and that they were eventually forced to seal the windows and blockade themselves within the palace walls from the ravenous swarm.

The feathered vermin stayed for many beads time until their presence began to quickly dwindle. Their abrupt disappearance was followed by violent thunderstorms accompanied by freezing rains with fantastic lightning shows. These shortly subsided, and all that was left where dark rolling clouds that covered the skies as far as the horizon, flashing brightly with silent sparks of blue lightning that illuminated the gloom.

Arriving next was a sea of fog as the clouds overhead slowly fell, floating lazily through the city like an ocean of mist; drifting slowly as it consumed the entire castle in it's ghostly vapors. The hazy streets were shrouded in a blurred twilight, and it was like living in a dream. The men bundled themselves in warm furs and sought comfort from the cold among the great fireplaces within the palace halls. Their breath became abnormally heavy and they noted that the firelight released a strange sheen, which made the air around them appear to glow.

With dread, they noticed that the water level of their wells had began to drop at an alarming rate. They filled all the barrels they could find to store the precious liquid, not wishing to leave the walls of the city to find any distant streams in the consuming darkness that lay beyond. Even with extra lengths of rope, their pails eventually hit bottom, until finally, all of the waterholes within the city ran dry.

Some of the men started to become hysterical, as everyone tried to keep their sanity in this strange existence. Slowly, the fog dissipated, and as the curious paintings described, they had witnessed that the sky was filled with countless numbers of bright glowing lights, appearing like distant twinkling candles across the heavens that touched the horizon in every direction. From that moment, many of the men locked themselves within their chambers for fear of these unknown sights and refused to venture outside. Strangely enough, the weather cleared and it became ever warmer, and they were able to venture into the city streets, however, the darkness of the land beyond the great walls kept them sealed within its borders.

The Elders were unable to guess why the record suddenly ended, for there were no more paintings thereafter to record what had followed, as the colorful murals abruptly ceased; leaving only a blank plaster wall and unused paint to illustrate their final sacrifice. Their people searched the city high and low, but every last warrior in their group had apparently disappeared without a single trace.

There were speculations among the citizens that the men had gone insane; or likely had either murdered each other or ran off into the night. It was perplexing that no bodies were ever found and all of their personal belongings still sat neatly within their rooms. Securely locked away, they discovered only a slight portion of the rations stored had actually been used. It was estimated that the men only lasted a dozen bands before they had mysteriously vanished. Without further evidence, a sparse and unfinished mural was all that was left of their grim legacy.

Rumors again began to fly, stories of how living men had invaded the world of the dead without invitation and were turned into spirits themselves. Some said that the lights in the night sky they had witnessed were the glowing eyes of vengeful specters that stole them away to their ethereal lands. So much effort and resources had been spent towards this expedition, and the men involved had been chosen because of their strength and bravery to face this bizarre and remarkable unknown. Though in hindsight, such noble characteristics were ultimately proven useless against the shrouding darkness. The night had won.

A lengthy search had been conducted by all of the morning tribes, but not a single trace of any of the chosen warriors from the expedition had ever been found. Out of respect for these lost heroes, such contests were never held again, not even for entertainment. The paintings of this legend can still be seen in the main hall of Silistra's illustrious Palace. The bare space left upon the opposite wall was covered in with the tribal brands of each member in honor of their memory.

*   *   *

Attempting to return to the valley above, the young misfits made their way back to the edge of the tunnel as Tara tried to push Lela up the rope, while he frequently peered behind them in fright. She cried out as their rope suddenly gave way and they were left bracing themselves upon a thin cleft. Far above, a weak area in the vine had snapped. They tried to grasp the shaft walls as best they could to keep from falling while the rest of their rope tumbled past them onto the landing a dozen feet below.

"What should we do now?" Lela cried.

"Do I look like a fortuneteller to you? Try to climb up if you can!" Tara stressed.

"I can't without the rope, the walls are too smooth," the girl whined as she couldn't find any handholds within reach. It was obvious she was right, there was no way back up without the cable to aid them. They had put too much strain on its bindings by attempting to climb up together in their haste to escape.

"I guess we will just have to go the other way," Tara suggested.

"Where? Down there with those ...*things*?" she screeched with rejection at his crazy proposition.

"No, this tunnel continues onward past the pit," he stated while trying to calm her nerves. They cautiously descended to the curved level of the tunnel once again, and retrieved the shredded remnants of their rope. With caution, they proceeded past the dark hole in haste, as if in fear that something was going to suddenly reach out and grab them. The worried youths continued on through the tunnel as it opened further, to their relief but resumed its ever downward run.

"What were those things, Tara?" the gypsy girl asked with unease.

"I was going to ask you the same thing," the boy responded, "but they were so far below, I don't think there is any way they could reach us up here."

"You don't think so? That is probably why the corridor we entered was blocked with debris, likely to keep those things from crawling out!" Lela flashed back. Tara tried not to think of the cave drawings of the thin black creatures with white eyes he had seen in the valley earlier. Apparently they *could* crawl out of there, and it had happened before.

The tunnels branched off and they left a trail of glowing lichen behind them as they continued through the weaving corridors of the cave. They noticed strange crystals and translucent rocks sticking through the cavern walls. The odd niches they saw before were even more evident here. To keep them from becoming completely lost, Lela continued to mark the walls with her shells.

Tara thought it was an unnecessary effort because this would probably be a one-way trip; and with a heavy heart, Lela began to think he was probably right, be the outcome good or bad.

The cold air was making their hands go numb, so they continually warmed them next to the burning seed. They had only brought a few of the firefruits with them but of course, they hadn't planned for this situation.

"Tara, I'm getting cold," Lela shivered as she rubbed her shoulders, attempting to shed the creeping chill.

"Here, put this on," he motioned, taking his outer robe off to cover Lela, only to noticed that it fluttered slightly as he handed it to her. When he held up his hand, Tara felt a soft breeze caress his skin. The cool wind became notably stronger as they entered into a large cavern farther down the passageway. A wide underground river ran straight through the middle of it, though he noticed the stream was unusually quiet, hardly making a ripple upon its glassy surface.

The cavern opened up into many other large passages. He was guessing by now that they were at about the same level as the area they had seen from the breach above. Tara raced up the bank trying to find a way across the river. As he peered within, the water seemed amazingly clear. He couldn't tell its speed but the stream didn't look very deep at all, so he suggested wading through it.

"Oh, I wouldn't go in there if I were you," Lela informed him with a hint of precaution.

"I don't want to, but we might not have any other choice," Tara admitted. Lela approached the riverbank a few feet away from him.

"Purified water is very clear like this, and it distorts your vision. The bottom may look extremely close, but it's actually much deeper than that," she warned. The river ran down the length of the cavern and into the darkness beyond. He tested her theory by attempting to grasp a large pebble near the bank of the water, but found that he could not reach it; noting the reflection of his hand in the water was sharply skewed. He quickly pulled away, puzzled by the illusion as he dried off his hands.

"Take a look that way, and I'll go over here," Tara pointed towards opposite ends of the stream. He didn't want to get separated, but this subterranean room was big enough that they could see each other at some distance.

The boy found a broken stalagmite farther down his side of the creek that laid across the river, creating a natural bridge upon which they could cross. He ran back to Lela at the other end of the cavern. She was crouching beside the riverbank, closely inspecting something in its depths. In the shadows beyond her, Tara thought he saw the walls move ...but then he saw their eyes.

Several tall creatures had silently swarmed out around her, though she still hadn't noticed. He cried out just as Lela let out a squeal that echoed throughout the cavern. The creatures backed away from her in defense as she flailed her torch wildly about; those closest to her cowering while shielding their eyes from the blazing light of the flaming seed with their long thin arms, while the others tried to apprehend the girl.

Tara ran to help her, but something struck him hard in the side and he dropped to the ground in pain. He lifted up his torch to see where the blow had come from and saw several more of the ugly creatures had come out of a side passage that he had failed to notice before.

A few held up stones they let fly, one missed, closely grazing his arm while he shielded his head as he tried to get back onto his feet. He stumbled from the blow and slipped on the wet bank, and fell headlong into the icy waters. The river was swift, and Lela had been right about it being much deeper. It was lucky for him that the fireseed torch he held continued to burn as it sizzled beneath the surface. The swift waters rushed him back towards the fallen stalactite and he reached out for it in desperation when he drew near.

The surface of the stone was too smooth and the column itself far too thick to get a proper hold of, and the boy was reluctant to release the torch so he could grasp it with both hands. Tara clung there for a brief moment until his fingers slipped free and he was swiftly carried downstream into the darkness beyond. He could hear Lela screaming his name as he sunk beneath the surface of the cool waters.

Only moments prior, Lela had thought she had seen something floating in the water and took a moment to take a closer inspection. She had failed to detect the quiet footsteps as the creatures as they surrounded her, but it was their peculiar airy breathing that alarmed her to their presence. She had screamed for Tara and swung her torch around her protectively to ward them off, and for a brief moment, they seemed to keep a respective distance.

The strange beings were actually much taller than a normal man but only seemed shorter than they were because the creatures had a habit of walking with their legs strangely bent forward. They all had hairless black skin with various patches of gray akin to freckles and age spots. Their eyes were large and reflected eerily in the torchlight. Both their arms and legs were longer than usual, as were their hands that were equally stretched. Their mouths were wide, which only gave them a ghoulish appearance as they spoke in whispers.

She had seen Tara running towards her, but watched as he fell into the river when she glanced back in his direction. The torch he held hadn't snuffed out while he was momentarily submerged but from his position, Tara couldn't appreciate the full effect it caused. The refracted light in the pure water caused a whole section of the river to glow as the torchlight was magnified and lit up the entire cavern. She could see Tara clearly now, flopping in the stream as he struggled to get ashore. The girl knew it was rare for anyone to learn how to swim, and she feared for his life.

The creatures were now approaching closer, and she tried desperately to ward them off with her flailing torch. There were just too many of them, and one finally managed to knock the flaming brand from her grasp with a hurled stone and they quickly seized her. Through the swarm of ghouls, she could see Tara drifting out of sight down the glowing river as the light slowly faded and he disappeared downstream into the unforgiving darkness.

Tara felt something lift him out from the freezing water as he choked and gasped for air. He had thrashed helplessly in the strong current that sucked him under a low rock wall and into an adjacent cavern. He looked around him as a dozen of the grayish creatures were lifting him out of the water with a woven net. He could only manage enough strength to cough up water and gag for air while entangled within the mesh.

He was held down by a score of cold clammy hands until he ceased struggling, and was swiftly hauled away to a small room that appeared to be formed from liquid stone. He was forced to stay there, shivering in the dark. Tara noticed there was a faint light of glowing lichen on the walls, which allowed him to view his surroundings.

His torch had also been recovered, but burned its way through the thin net and dropped back into the river, only to be washed away downstream in the rushing waters. The whispering beasts came back to escort him through a long tunnel. The strange glowing moss which grew in patches everywhere was bright enough for him to find his way, although he stumbled many times on the slippery path. Tara noticed that the lichen glowed slightly brighter whenever he passed near a patch of fungus. He finally realized that the plants didn't react to light but responded to heat, even what little of it there was radiating from his shivering body.

Surrounding them were a mass of exotic constructs. They appeared to be cocoons at first, as if they were formed of white clay, designed in strange flowing cascades, almost as if it were mud that had been frozen in its tracks and hollowed out to make chambers. He was taken to a shallow pit and thrown inside. It was apparently some sort of seat because it was only knee-deep. The lanky creatures slowly shambled back up to a large round building stationed above him, its structure supported upon an array of thin flowing columns.

Tara noticed how eerily graceful these dark beings were when they climbed upon the walls. 'So that was what those niches were for, which were perfectly distanced for their long spidery limbs,' he realized. The windows of the building above gave off a ghostly blue light. Tara's attention guided back to the alien creatures that stood around, staring at him. Another of the man-things came out of the building and examined him closely. He was near enough to hear it speak and he could swear he heard the creature say 'Surface dweller' or something close to that remark.

Tara was placed near a strange translucent rock that glowed with a soft inner light. It gave off no heat at all that he could tell, but the orange stone had somehow dried off his clothes in a short span of time. Curious about this, he moved to touch it but his hand was quickly slapped away with a painful swat by a short rod held by one of the creatures. Tara rubbed his bruised hand, not wishing to test the guard's patience.

He was again placed in a net and carried along a series of dangerous slopes and treacherous passageways, up sheer cavern walls and across narrow clefts through numerous chambers on their precarious journey. The boy was amazed to the sheer extent of the cave system that weaved throughout this underground labyrinth.

He was terribly worried about Lela, wondering what had happened to her. He was eventually dropped, quite unceremoniously, into a heap on the floor within the presence of an aged being that held its walking staff in a threatening manner. The creature then silently motioned the others to have the boy untied. After he was left alone with the creature, the thing sniffed and grunted at him.

"*Pro missse u won't hert usss?*" It wheezed in a questioning tone, Tara was caught off guard for a moment, bewildered by its request.

"Uh ...no, I won't hurt you," he responded, slightly perplexed by the question.

"*Yy uu coomasstt heer?*" It hissed, coming nearer, as Tara struggled to understand what it was trying to say.

"Why did I come here...?" he tried to decipher with a shrug of his shoulders, "We got stuck down here. My friend and I were trying to find a way out of the valley above as we were trapped inside by the cliff walls and we

couldn't find a way out," he finished, hoping his words
made sense. The creature slowly paced around him in a
familiar human way.   Tara asked the hunched being,
"There was a girl with me, where is she now?"

The thing just turned to stare at him with its large pale
eyes, making Tara feel quite uncomfortable. He was
about to repeat the question once again, when the old
creature hobbled off abruptly into the darkness. It came
back shortly with a few glowing rocks, some squirming
fish, and a few odd plants set upon a flat slate, and the
boy was motioned to eat. Tara tried chewing the white
leaves first, but they were bland and tasteless. He just
couldn't bring himself to eat the raw fish, which
continued to twitch upon his plate, and he had absolutely
no idea what to do with the luminous turquoise stones
left on the platter.

After a time, the scrawny creature seemed satisfied and
motioned the boy to follow him. They approached a hole
in the cavern wall that ascended for a small distance
beyond.   The old creature climbed through the tiny
crawlspace with ease but Tara had a rough time of it,
finding the walls were too smooth for his hands to get a
grip as he stumbled behind. The passage blossomed into
a large room, which was surrounded with thick glass-like
walls. Here, strange images could be seen through the
contorting sheets of crystal.

There were mural paintings about the room on the other
side, much like the pictographs he had learned to read
from his father. Lying on the floor below them were
several leather pouches, old rotted tunics, and other
familiar items of gear that anyone might carry.   His
attention was guided to the drawings. There were the
symbols of the dark skinned long-armed beings he was

now familiar with, and of normal men being taken to caverns below ground. Among them were drawings of rock formations and strange crystals, and other things he didn't understand. There were several indications that the artist dreamed of the sun, and drew himself as a desert tribesman.

The ancient creature before him touched a glowing stone against a translucent wall, and the boy watched in awe as it slowly illuminated. Within, Tara could see the form of a man, long dead and embedded deep in the crystal's thick distorted glass. His still body was wearing heavy furs and a tunic embossed with an emblem that signified the city of Silistra. The boy had frequently seen this symbol before, marked on his fathers' maps and upon the city gates when they had visited the ancient palace nearly half a cycle ago.

As the creature continued to cast glowing stones on other slits within the crystal walls, the boy could see they held many similar corpses captured in frozen horror. The withered being came to stare him in the face with its large emotionless eyes.

"*Uu nott leevv eetherrr...*" it whispered coldly.

Chapter 9

The evening seasons would be coming soon, and many of the noon tribes began departing the city of Hagda on their ceaseless trek to follow the sun. Lela's tribe had long since departed the metropolis and Dooroo found himself left without a leader, let alone the Torg's missing son. There wasn't much left for his tribe to do but move on. The disappearance of their clan chief was just as mysterious as his vanishing son. As for the tribe, the migration must continue; for the sun waits for no man.

After much contemplation, Dooroo finally decided to elect a younger fellow as their temporary chief. If Torg did not show up to assume his position soon, his station would become forfeit. Most clans had strict rules about leadership, for they believed the position was so reserved that only those who were the brightest could hope to achieve its seat. They further believed that only those who could recognize that their title was a genuine handle of responsibility, and not for the purposes of petty abuse of power, should ever be allowed to hold such a respected place in their tribe. Any clansmen in such a post who displayed a severe lack of ethics were quickly dealt with in the most permanent of ways.

As the noon tribes left, teams from the evening season clans began to swarm into Hagda, who were promptly informed of the arcane relics as the other tribe leaders were before them. This was a mystery set to solving, though many citizens remembered the tales of those few heroes who had wandered off into the night. The taboos and superstitious fears of the dark eluded all reason in their culture. For many of their people, even murky shadows were avoided like a haunted childhood dream.

*   *   *

Tara was released back into the guards, which he termed as a tribe of Shadowmen. The children were enslaved into laboring for the creatures that had captured them. There was little prospect of escape, since they were hopelessly lost within the maze-like labyrinth of this bizarre underground world. Oddly, there were few enough shadowmen that could speak their verbal language in its most basic form. What they could not translate in words, they did so with crude attempts using sign language.

At first, they both believed these grotesque men to be nothing but monsters but were impressed by the level of culture that was exhibited among their people. Tara became well acquainted with one elderly clansman named Gree, who helped teach him their methods of living below ground. He was told that the high elder of their Shadow tribes was an over a dozen cycles old, from what Tara could estimate; though, down here in the constant darkness, the passage of time was not measured.

Gree informed him they would not be allowed back to the surface above because they were afraid of retaliation. Their history had shown that men from the surface had always treated them with extreme prejudice, which quickly escalated into violence by invading their subterranean territories and brutally slaughtering their people. Through much effort, Tara tried to get the point across that the people of the surface did not know of their existence, and that they could possibly come to common grounds if the surface dwellers and the shadow tribes could meet in peace. Though the boy tried to validate his claim, his opinions were only scoffed at.

Tara's eyes never really got accustomed to the dark as keenly as his hosts but when he stayed in any particular area; his higher body temperature caused the luminous moss to shine brightly, which allowed him safe passage. The youngsters soon discovered there were many levels they were unable to access simply because they did not possess such long limbs as these creatures.

There were a great many caverns full of fungi, including giant insects that were herded like cattle. They saw massive raw metal structures and other frameworks that aided in transportation to and from the lower caverns. These creatures used the curious orange rocks for smelting metals without fire and possessed chisels comprised of a strange obsidian stone that could carve away solid rock as though it were soft wood. The rivers were used to deliver all sorts of provisions and tools by packing them into immense watertight gourds they transported by an ingenious system of underground streams. Tara tried to become familiar with the confusing puzzle of hallways and rivers but was only accustomed to life on the open plains, not worming his way through dark and musty tunnels. It was obvious that Lela became more distressed as time passed. She warned Tara that nightfall would soon cover the surface, and when that happened they could be sure of never being rescued from this dark hell.

On several occasions, the children had attempted to escape from their captors as they fled blindly through the tunnels, but they were eventually cornered at some dead-end or impassable chasm. Strangely, they were never restrained nor punished for such conduct as they would have rightly expected. Apparently, knowing that they were hopelessly trapped within this massive underground labyrinth was punishment enough.

Tara was amazed at the considerable size of the communities within these shadow tribes, and like those above, sometimes they fought. They even witnessed brief excursions by neighboring cavern dwellers, but they lacked any banners or uniforms, and Tara could never tell their clans apart. This subterranean existence was beginning to make Tara feel dispirited and mentally unglued, while Lela had her off moments herself from time to time as well. Gree tried to persuade them to settle their minds and that they should just try to be happy with their new life here, despite Tara's many attempts of describing the surface world to him.

"*Sometimesse we surfacee when there isss darknesss,*" Gree stated with his slithering voice.

"At night? But there's nothing alive on the surface then, besides, you would freeze to death," the boy responded.

"*Many more thingsss alive than you knoww. Wee gatherrr wood and deaddd brush from abuvvv to fertalize our gardensss,*" Gree related.

"I heard stories of our stone cities and villages being destroyed on the surface during nightfall. Was it your people who did this?" Tara inquired.

"*Noo, not miine, but perhapsss suum uuther tribe,*" Gree denied under the accusing eyes of the child.

"But why would they do that? I've been trying to tell you that we never knew of your existence," he blurted with a heavy sigh along with a tinge of exasperation glinting in his eyes; then Tara remembered the cave drawings he saw in the valley above, "...well, except for the jungle tribe that we came across. What happen to them?" the boy inquired.

"*They burrowed intoo our hiive, thay throw fire, we only defend ourselvesss*," Gree related with finality, while trying to explain that their Shadow Tribes were strict xenophobes, which was a concept Tara could not understand in the slightest.

Gree taught them how to harvest the fungi and to fish with their curiously efficient fan nets, and how to cook their meals using the remarkable orange rocks. Though Gree could not come to understand why the youths would always insist on cooking their food. Gree thought live wiggling fish tasted just fine.

The couple was offered a large shell fashioned from clay as their private accommodations whenever they were moved about the system of caves, which happened frequently. Lela was certain this was done to keep them both confused as to their location. Planning ahead, they had secretly saved up many beads worth of edible rations and continued to make plans for their escape; even if their past efforts had proven to be in vain.

They had also collected several of the blue stones that gave off a modest amount of heat, which helped keep them comfortably warm in these cool tunnels. The odd orange cooking stones were usually too large in size to be carried. Nonetheless, he noticed the beings took great care never to actually touch one with their bare hands. He experimented once with a meal of fish and plopped it directly onto the surface of the strange rock to see if it would bake faster. To his surprise, the fish instantly turned the color of ash and became as dry as a bone. Obviously these crystal rocks were not to be played with! From then on, he kept a respectable distance from these strange stones.

After a time, Lela became quite efficient with a fan net

to catch fish and cultivating the fungi. When she wasn't forced to work, Lela secretly made torches fashioned from large fish bones and strips of dead moss with the cloth from her skirt. With a stroke of luck, Gree, who was seemingly unimpressed with their personal items, casually mentioned where their firefruit and weapons were being kept.

This was the break Tara had been waiting for; they had spent too much time in the past running through the dim caverns trying to find a way out. His shikar was a formidable weapon and might prove useful in their venture to escape, and he did not wish to leave it behind. Apparently, Gree wasn't of stout mind and Lela cleverly weaseled information out of him about the passages on the upper levels. She learned how they frequently dug vents to the surface to let fresh air into the caverns.

They noticed that many of the shadowmen never bothered to approach or talk to either of them, treating the pair of strange-looking surface children as if they were freaks and oddities. There were also many scribbles above several passage doorways, Tara discovered these were writings that slowly described the sound of a word, instead of using a picture to depict a thing or event. He attempted to learn their written language from their guardian, but poor old Gree wasn't too terribly bright and he generally failed to help the boy grasp the knack of it. They both realized that there might come a time when circumstance may call for them to harm one of these creatures in order to reach the surface, and they weren't quite sure how they might react to that.

Their next break finally came when there befell a violent tremor throughout the caverns. Lela had been off tending the fungi plants when it hit, but she wasted no time to take advantage of this rare opportunity, despite the personal risk. While the shadowmen ran in fear of the falling rocks and cave-ins, she made for the crystal room that held their personal items. One guard eyed Lela suspiciously as she approached, and attempted to accost her but was suddenly struck down by a falling stalactite. She found their belongings wrapped in a bundle of soft dry moss. The firefruit didn't appear to be in terrible condition, for it seemed that the coolness of the caves had helped to preserve the seeds.

In another portion of the cavern, Gree had managed to pull Tara under a large cleft of rock and tried to explain that small tremors like this happen infrequently whenever some of their workers tunnel too close to pressurized streams or hot steam vents. Tara did his best to protect his head from the falling debris. The shadowmen had more to worry about, for though they were fairly tall, their lean stature made them quite frail and their bones were far more brittle than his.

When Gree noticed Lela running at them through the dust and falling rocks with a bundle of torches and a silver shikar held in her arms, he shook his head disapprovingly. Tara looked up to see her approaching and turned back to face Gree. Realizing Lela had taken the initiative, Tara knew what he had to do.

"Sorry about this, Gree," the boy announced with a sigh of apology, "but it's time for us to leave," and he squarely plastered Gree across the chin with a solid punch from his curled fist. Poor Gree almost seemed like he had expected they're betrayal before he crumbled to the ground, his head wobbling in disappointment before he blacked out.

Lela stopped to glance down at the comatose old man

and quickly handed Tara his sword. Through the clouds of gray dust and falling rocks, they made their way past the edge of the fungus crops and towards the ascending passages they hoped would lead them to the surface. They were unhampered as they ran through the shaking passages, for it seemed that the shadowmen had a hard time breathing in the dust-filled air. The young couple crossed their veils over their faces, as they were well accustomed to whenever their clans had faced fierce dust storms and blowing winds on the surface above. They had reached the passage that led to the upper levels but came to an abrupt halt when they found the shaft itself had completely caved in.

"Oh no, not again," Lela groaned in anguish.

Another short tremor shook and a vast fissure ripped along the side of the passage. Tara was beginning to get fairly worried, afraid they were both going to be buried alive. They wrapped their scarves tightly over their faces as boiling gases started to pour into the narrow corridor. They jumped the steaming crevasse and backtracked towards an adjacent hallway, which to their surprise, was not where it had once been. The shifting strata had sheared a section of the tunnel into a broken jumble of boulders and debris.

A geyser of boiling water sprayed into the large cavern they had just descended into. The surrounding lichen glowed so brightly it was almost blinding, then suddenly faded and withered away from the extreme heat as it died. The steam rose to the ceiling and instantly condensed to pour down as hot rain upon them. The excess vapor that shot into the adjacent caverns had caused the light patches of glowing moss to brighten considerably. Temporarily blinded, the few shadowmen lingering there, who had been cowering from the falling rocks, quickly covered their eyes and tumbled to the floor in agony.

Hand in hand, Lela pulled Tara into another cavern with a large running stream and they made their way to the river's edge, flinging away fan nets that lay scattered about the crude dock. As they pushed a huge gourd into the stream, one of the shadowmen grabbed Tara from behind and spun him around. The boy swung his unlit torch like a club and caught the creature square in the face. Lela jumped into the floating gourd and yelled to Tara over the noise of the rushing stream, as Tara barely managed to catch the lip of the container and pulled himself inside. She pinched him in the confined space.

"Now this seems familiar…" she giggled lightly.

'By the Sun Gods, leave it to her to make fun in a crisis!' Tara thought to himself with a smirk as he rolled his eyes. The gourd rushed downstream with a mix of debris that shook loose from the river docks. Tara tried the best he could to secure the lid and keep the cold water out but unfortunately, these giant gourds were designed to be sealed from the outside.

The river rocked and jolted them as their makeshift boat struck overhangs and banged along the sides of the bank. At one point, the gourd nearly rolled over and practically half filled with water. They knew they were being washed farther along than they desired and if a neighboring shadow tribe caught them, then their fate would be all too precarious. The waterlogged gourd picked up speed as it suddenly entered a side stream, while their fragile capsule bobbed and swayed through the tight subterranean passages.

Suddenly, the side of the gourd split open with a jolting

smash, and more water came gushing into the shell. They were forced to abandon their fractured ship on a muddy shoreline littered with large pillars of stone. This place did not look familiar to them in any sense.

Through the surrounding tunnels, they could hear a howling wind as it whistled through dozens of hidden gaps and dark fissures. Their seed torches were wet but lit quickly despite the fact. The tremors did not seem to reach this region of the caverns but they knew it wouldn't be long before the shadow creatures would come looking for them in numbers. The two worried companions found themselves completely lost, for the passages they had hoped to escape through were left far behind at the breached geysers. There was nothing left to do but try to find a way out, and they would have to do so quickly.

Tara had learned from Gree that many new tunnels had recently been opened to the surface to allow in fresh air, and in turn, permitted dangerous gasses to escape. The curious boy had inquired about these phenomena, but Gree wasn't very helpful, saying it was merely air you could not breathe. Unfortunately, Lela had twisted her ankle when they had crashed against the rocks near the shore and had to favor her wounded leg, so Tara helped her along as best he could. They looked for any sign of ascending passages but it was apparent that they were only heading deeper underground. There were no writings or cryptic symbols along the passage walls in this cavern. They had guessed that this area was uninhabited, most likely because of the excessive amount of deep mud they had to trample through in the vicinity of this forgotten grotto.

They found a lone boulder in the middle of the vast mudflat and took the opportunity for a short rest while they sat to enjoy a meal from their meager rations. It was the only spot of dry ground in this lake of mud that they could find. Tara wedged his torch into a crack in the rock and took a seat beside Lela, who was looking quite distraught.

"When is this mud going to end?" she complained while attempting to remove the muck from her legs with a length of her tattered veils, but it only managed to cling to the material instead.

"I tried to find something to sketch on, but there's nothing down here to draw with. Gree told me they made maps with their written language, but I couldn't make any sense out of those scribbles he showed me," Tara sighed as he scraped his shikar across the boulder to clean its blade while gazing around at their cheerless surroundings. The blaze from their torch reached out to light the cavern, but the walls were so distant that it only faded away into darkness. The two youths just sat there in the quiet gloom, pondering their unhappy fate.

"Do you hear something Tara? Listen ...there!" Lela pointed out into the shadows. A gale had picked up somewhere in the cave a faint breeze whistled to them from the distant darkness.

"If it's a way out of this mess we have got to try for it," Tara stated eagerly as he tried to kick off some of the caked mud from his feet, but realizing that he would only have to wade back into the mire surrounding them.

They couldn't stay still for long as the cold mud was beginning to numb their muscles. They abandoned their dry oasis and tromped through the mush until their feet suddenly gave way underneath them. Tara could barely feel the stone floor beneath the tips of his toes. There was no way they could move through this neck-high muck, so they back-tracked until they reached the cavern wall and made their way along its edge towards the sound of rushing air overhead.

As they approached, their light revealed a tunnel high above, while appreciating that the steep climb would be treacherous. They could see vapors rushing through the crevice which swirled and clung to the ceiling like lamp smoke. Tara could not see any way to climb the mud-caked walls, and the foul grime that covered them from head to toe certainly wouldn't help his grip. He was shocked when Lela leapt upon the wall and began to climb.

"What are you doing, you'll fall!" Tara warned, trying to pull her back.

"Look around, Tara, there's nowhere else to go," she vented suddenly, "light another seed torch and give it to me, I have an idea."

Tara un-strapped another fire seed while igniting it with his own torch and handed it to her. Lela dug her hand into the muddy wall and pulled out a clump, she then stuffed the blazing seed into the hole she had just made. She was baking the mud under the intense heat of the firefruit torch.

"I hope this works," she whispered.

The stiffened mud cooled quickly while she dug another step above, and Tara noticed it resembled the niches the shadowmen used. Progress was slow, but she eventually scaled herself all the way up the slippery sheer wall. When she reached the top, Lela found a solid anchor and wrapped their frail rope around Tara as he climbed up in case the fragile steps failed to hold his weight.

The portal that made itself so difficult to reach was worth the climb, for it beheld a spectacular sight. They had breached the lip of a vast cavern filled with a maze of geysers shooting from oddly shaped pillars of brightly hued rock, which were colored in every imaginable shade from the mixture of mineral deposits that seeped from their vents. The ceiling itself could not be seen, for huge clouds of steam and thick vapor flowed violently above them. They were just happy to get out of the mud and tried vainly to clean each other off while they held one another closely to keep warm. It had been a long time since they had escaped their captors and they took a moment to gather some much-needed rest.

When they finally awoke, Lela assumed they might have slept far longer than she had first thought, for their firefruit torches had nearly burned out. Perhaps its extended storage in the caves had dried the seeds out more than they had assumed, and now they only had two left in their possession. She shook Tara until he awoke and they flaked off the dried mud from their skin and clothing.

The heat from the geysers caused vast patches of moss to glow brightly, allowing them to see unhampered. They carefully secured their vine rope to an outcropping and cautiously climbed down to the landing, lest it break on them like it had before. This time, however, they had to leave their rope behind since there was no way to unfasten it from the perch above where they had entered.

The temperature in this massive cavern was much more agreeable, but they avoided the steaming waterspouts and mineral pools with care. Lela stopped short at the edge of a tranquil green pool with a bank that was dyed with hints of bright yellow and turquoise. She suddenly grabbed Tara's arm to stop him as he tried to continue past her.

"What are you doing?" he marked in confusion.

"Hold on, Tara, my uncle once showed me a natural hot spring just off the shores of the Eon Sea," the gypsy girl replied while she picked up a large rock and lobbed it at the bank of the pool, "he once told me about a tribe who had lost several pack animals loaded with supplies while crossing near the shore of a hot spring," she finished as the stone hit the ground by the bank of the pool.

The stone cracked the top layer as it broke through the thin surface of what had seemed like perfectly solid ground, and plopped into the boiling water simmering beneath. The astonished boy raised his eyebrows in shock; he could have been scalded alive! He was beginning to think that members of the mountain tribes, like Lela's, led much more interesting lives than his.

"It looks like we will just have to find a way around this. If we had a long pole we could use it to test the ground, because these fragile mineral shelves aren't always the same color," Lela advised.

There was hardly a chance of finding any wood or branches down here to use as a pole, and Tara began to yearn for the makeshift spear he had left behind in the jungle valley before they committed their act of lunacy by climbing down into this world of shadows. They gathered as many loose stones they could find along the way and pitched them towards any surface they thought suspicious. Tara nearly jumped out of his pants when passing next to the geyser vents, as they would erupt without notice and shot gouts of steam in spontaneous bursts. They eyed watermarks upon the rock walls that betrayed the fact that there were times when the level of the boiling waters within would rise much higher, so they hurried on their way.

The humidity caused Lela's muddy veils to cling to her shapely body, while Tara managed to wash off most of the dirt from his robes by scrubbing them in a warm shallow pool. After redressing, he felt uncomfortably wet, and some of the minerals in the water not only smelled unpleasant but also made his skin itch terribly.

The air was misty but well lit by the glowing moss, so they didn't need to use their precious few torches. After cleaning up the best they could, the young couple set out to search for an exit. Unfortunately, the colossal cavern they now occupied refused to offer any hint towards that end. Curiously, there were areas that resembled formed pathways running between the geysers, but this could have been a trick of the light.

They finally made their way down the center of the subterranean steam beds, passing several clumped gardens of oversized fungus plants and shards of crystals, having grown to an unnatural size most likely due to the extra moisture and unusual minerals present in these waters. Given that fact, they weren't too surprised to find the water here was tart with a metallic taste and thoroughly undrinkable, and there certainly weren't any fish to be seen as they made their way along the banks.

Lela spotted something up ahead as they came upon a circle of enormous boulders that seemed purposely placed. As they approached closer, they could see that these large square stones, which were twice their height, had been carved into the shapes of maniacal grinning heads. The figures seemed quite human, each bearing a stern look upon their petrified faces. The statues were arranged so that they all looked outward from their center where there lay a deep foreboding pit.

The stone here was moist, and Tara slumped carefully to

the ground as he nearly slipped while trying to peer down into the dark hole. Lela was admiring the quality of the carvings, running her hands along the wet surface of the rock, wondering why Shadowmen would even bother to carve the faces of surface dwellers, since they apparently didn't much care for them.

Tara stood back from the sloping edge and tossed a stone into the dark hole, but he didn't hear it hit bottom or even bounce along the walls of the pit. He shrugged and turned back to Lela as she gently caressed the ancient statue in wonder. She turned her head once to glance at Tara then made a retake as she jerked back around. Through the heavy mist, Lela had thought she saw the air move behind him. Her eyes widened in shock as she saw something rise out of the hole, looming above him.

"Tara! Behind you!" she screamed to him through the thick air. He turned to see a huge slug-like creature ooze out of the pit, the small rock he had thrown just a moment before was currently stuck to the side of the grotesque stump that was its head.

The size of the slug was frightening, for it was nearly twice as high as the stone boulders around them and several times their length. Even worse, was that after the monstrosity came free of the burrow; a second one emerged behind it. Tara ran to Lela as they hid behind the statues, hoping the boulders were placed close enough together to keep the beasts trapped inside.

They were dreadfully disappointed to their assumption, as the two children screamed in unison when the first slimy creature slowly oozed its way over the carved rock where they were hiding. They jumped out of the way just as it plopped to the ground as the other slug behind it squeezed between the stone heads in pursuit. In a moment of brave stupidity, Tara lunged forward to gash the slug with his silver sword. It ripped through its flesh like thick soup from which began to ooze a darker substance from the wound, but otherwise, the creature was apparently unharmed for it didn't react whatsoever to the severe cut it had suffered.

The creature was still attacking and flexed an oval mouth, ringed with a batch of horrible jagged teeth, its orifice so large that it could swallow a grown man whole. Tara imagined himself for a moment, floating in the transparent guts of the thing heaving before him. That image was enough to turn his heels and flee with renewed urgency.

As the monster lunged for him, its head came down faster than he would have thought possible. Swinging the sword in a wide arc, he managed to lop off one of its four eyestalks; whereupon it instantly withdrew the amputated stump into its head as if it were never there. They both turned and jolted for the mineral pools to make their escape. The slugs were slow for their relative size but could easily keep up with their smaller prey.

The young couple hopped their way through the precarious sulfur beds along the mineral ledges until they suddenly found themselves blocked; surrounded by several deep mineral pools sparkling with tranquil hues. Considering wading across to their salvation, Tara attempted to stick his foot in the waters but pulled it back in a sudden yelp of pain. The sapphire blue waters were scalding hot despite the deceptive lack of any steam rising from its surface. They tried to circle back but it was too late, the slugs had blocked their only avenue of escape. The only option left was to climb a dead and hardened waterspout at the center of the small isle, to what Tara considered would only be a convenient height to be attacked by these monstrosities.

The walkway they had taken was constricted, though the huge slugs required a much wider surface to tread upon. The towering beasts stopped short as their sides touched the blistering pool, just shy of reaching them. The creatures backed away to try another approach to gain access to this fresh meal that had so conveniently trapped itself. Lela and Tara held each other on their delicate perch as they watched in a mix of dread and astonishment as to what the slugs did next.

Acting in cooperation, one slug blocked their escape as the other swallowed up huge mounds of wet mud from the ground nearby; they could see the sludge clumped within its semi-transparent body. The giant slugs then switched places as one regurgitated the mud onto the narrow pathway, while the other continued to gather more soil. They continued this process without rest as they widened the path to reach their quarry, all the while, Lela hopelessly searched around them as if some sort of escape route would magically appear.

Eventually, one of the creatures became impatient with this maneuver and coursed over their crude pile of muck before the path was complete, trying to flatten it out and to be the first one to get to their trapped prey. Lela screamed as it made its bulk over the narrow hurdle, coming within an arm's length of them. It slipped, however, on the excess of its own regurgitated slime, and was unable to stop itself as it slowly slid into the hot springs, where it thrashed violently before it sank into the dark blue depths of the pool beyond their sight. A horrid stench of boiled slug filled the air around them.

The other creature watched its comrade scald itself to

death with disinterest, driven only by its hunger to the meal within reach. It rushed forward across the barrier while Tara readied their defense. For an encouraging moment, it began to appear as though their hopes would come true, as the second beast also began to slide into the hot pool. One side of the slug slipped partly into the water where it immediately began to bubble, but the beast lunged forward with renewed vigor from the pain.

In a desperate move, Tara shielded Lela as he slashed open the side of the creatures face when it came within reach. The beast opened its wide oval mouth to swallow Tara from above, and would have succeeded, but in its convulsion to suck Tara in, it could only regurgitate the pile of dirt in its throat that it had forgotten to release in its haste to reach them. Tara was knocked from Lela's side and he fell to the edge of the basin as he was showered in sticky mud and slime. His right leg splashed for but a moment into the scalding water where he fell. He screamed in pain and pulled it out quickly, trying to remove the pant leg that was now soaked with the blistering hot mineral water.

The slug, now free of its discharge, leaned down to engulf him. Lela screamed at Tara while he struggled with his leg, and having no time to think, all he could do was splash water from the pool at the slug with the blade of his sword. It flinched as the scalding water hit one of the creature's eye stems, sucking it back into its head in response. Tara could not tell if his attacks were effective, for the beast was hideously silent.

His leg hurt terribly and the skin had turned bright pink from the burn, but he barely managed to crawl out of the way just before the monster's head came crashing down. The beast took a huge bite of mud from the spot where

Tara had fallen. After an eerie moment, it spat out the thick mud, realizing its prey had moved.

It raised its head again, but Tara was now trapped at the edge of the geyser spout just below Lela's perch. There was no way around the slug, the monster was just too large and there was no possible means for him to climb over its slimy body. He glanced up for a brief moment with an expression of forlorn towards her, but Lela was hidden behind the rim of the spout. He was stuck and there was no way he could reach her.

The slugs' massive mouth came down to suck him up into its gelatinous gut. Tara held up his shikar and closed his eyes, only hoping that his fancy sword would make this meal highly uncomfortable for the creature. There was a flash of light from above and the sound of sizzling flesh as Lela lit a firefruit, and flung it headlong into the open mouth of the beast.   The slug reeled about feverishly, for it had sucked the torch deep within its gut that now glowed eerily from within. It tried to spit the stem up, but the fireseed refused to dislodge from its throat as the monster continued to thrash about wildly.

The beast's frantic lurching finally caused it to lose purchase on the slick ground, and it slowly slipped into the pool to join its companion. The shaken couple watched in silence as the glowing slug, radiating light from the fiercely burning torch within its transparent body, sank to incredible depths until its eerie illumination was finally smothered by the gloom.

Chapter 10

Lela bound Tara's injured leg with strips of cloth torn from her dress. He cursed uncontrollably until she finished packing the bandage with cold mud, but Tara eventually quieted down from sheer exhaustion. They praised their luck that there weren't any more monstrosities in that pit and Tara made a promise to himself that he would never go throwing rocks down mysterious holes ever again.

"By the Sun Gods, you were lucky, I almost dropped my flint trying to light that torch," she confessed while cleaning the sticky mud from her hands. Honestly, Tara felt anything but fortunate ...ever since this unfortunate escapade began, though he took a humbled moment to apologize for yelling at Lela, and kissed her gently upon the cheek in sincere appreciation for her kindness.

The fishbone torches she had smuggled away were now covered with so much muck as to be useless, and they now had only one fireseed left to spare. They stumbled along the best they could, exploring farther down into the cavern. The heavy stench of minerals was beginning to make them sick, so they tried as they could to find another way out. The geysers cluttering the massive cavern seemed to stretch on forever as the chamber parted into several vast canyons. Unfortunately, the quickest routes towards the surface also happened to be the most precarious, and Tara didn't care to chance slipping off the path and getting boiled alive.

To their surprise, they found more ancient ruins built alongside the cavern walls covered with handcrafted stonework that must have been hundreds of cycles old. Fitted together were blocks of enormous size, the workmanship of it was astonishing. Carving out the rock would have been an easy affair from what Tara had seen the way shadowmen had used their strange black chisels, but how they could manage to lift such massive blocks into place was beyond his understanding.

At one intersection, they stumbled across a small tower built of stone within the middle of a large steaming pool. They could see through the shallow water that there was once a walkway to reach it but it was now thoroughly submerged. Lela was always eager for exploring and finding lost treasure but there was no safe passage to the isolated building. It didn't take Tara long to convince her that finding their way out of this mess, instead of searching for trinkets, was their most immediate concern at the moment. Even though the stench of the toxic minerals was making them ill, they quietly dreaded the moment they found another avenue; for the hot steam was the only thing causing the lichen to glow so brightly, and once they left this cavern, they would be committed to using their last torch.

Along one wall, Lela pointed out a portal that had been intentionally sealed, for within the short tunnel a flat blank wall emerged to greet them. Tara dug into this facade with his blade and found the plastering was so old that it easily fell away in brittle chunks. The makeshift barrier wasn't very thick and they forced their way through it into a much cooler tunnel that sported a low ceiling, which forced them to crouch as they proceeded.

There was a notable lack of luminous moss in this area so they both went back to scrape some of the lichen off the walls to take with them. However, they killed several of the glowing lichen in this manner, for the plants were quite fragile and they found that ripping its delicate roots from the stone only caused the plants to die off, and their glow quickly faded. They hunted around until they eventually found a small patch growing on a thin slate of rock which they could carry. It was a little heavy to bear but well worth it to keep their last fireseed in reserve.

They entered into the low tunnel and found that it split off into a virtual maze, with corridors going up, down, left, right, and even zigzagging without any clear direction. They entered several rooms that were also riddled with adjacent tunnels, however, they could not find one big enough to allow them to walk upright. The miniature passageways didn't look like natural formations in the least, and the maze of corridors seemed to lead absolutely nowhere. As they went deeper, they heard a sharp squawking cry echoing through the maze of tunnels. The source was difficult to pinpoint, but after much searching they eventually made their way closer to its location.

The passage itself became severely constricted until they were driven to crawl on their hands and knees, but they could tell even from their current distance that the area ahead was fairly well lit. They climbed out from the tight tunnel into a large room brightly illuminated by a number of white and orange crystals embedded within the walls. They found themselves stationed on a ledge high above the floor of the cavern, where they were hidden from view behind a cluster of small boulders from the gargantuan creature lurking within. There, in the rounded corner of the room, was what looked to be like a large bird with an enormous head. The features of this monstrosity appeared very similar to the stone totem they had seen when they had first entered the hidden valley on the surface above.

The huge beast lay among multitudes of small objects of what looked to be eggs spotted with brown and gray blotches, although, these were barely the width of a child's fist. The eggs were absurdly petite in size than one might imagine such a massive beast to lay. Lela pulled at Tara's sleeve and quietly pointed across the room to an opening below. From the tunnel mouth, small beings that looked like pygmy shadowmen were carrying in strips of fungus and other vegetation, and offering it to the large bird-beast.

The little men closely resembled their friend Gree, but were much shorter and compact, and bore strange bony knobs upon their heads. They fed the great bird without apparent fear even though the creature was so enormous that it could gobble up a few of them as a snack, if it was so inclined. From the burrow, a whole train of dwarf shadowmen continued to bring in great bundles of the fungus meal, and just as quickly, they scurried out through a little hole at the far end of the cavern. Looking around, Tara was trying to figure out how such a large animal could have gotten in here in the first place, as it was obvious there was no entrance that could fit its massive girth.

Tara was familiar with the orange stones that poked through the cavern walls, and the foggy white crystals appeared to be similar to the ones the Elder of the Shadow Tribe had used to light up the quartz walls when they were first captured. Tara began to assume that perhaps it might be the proximity of these stones to one another that caused them to glow so brightly. After close observation, he could tell that the short wings of the enormous beast had been trimmed, though he was certain that even if the creature were free of this cave that its exaggerated size and massive body would keep it from ever being able to take flight.

There was, unfortunately, no other way out of the room except through the tunnel from which the tiny men had withdrawn. Feeling hungry and exhausted, the two adolescents planned to make a rush for the small outlet in hopes of escape. The huge bird might be trained not to eat the little people, but he could imagine it was quite capable of biting off their heads if it became startled, and neither of them wanted to do anything to possibly encourage that end.

After its hearty meal of consuming the bed of moss it had been provided, the creature quieted down and appeared to rest soundly. The young couple took this opportunity to scamper down the wall towards the opposite tunnel. As he ran for the doorway, Tara faltered; dropping the moss-covered slate he was carrying as it clamored to the floor. The massive creature awoke and bleated loudly, and upon sighting the pair, it began flapping about frantically with its stubby wings and creating a commotion, squawking so loudly that it hurt their ears, although it didn't make any attempt to attack them directly.

Tara dove through the small entrance as Lela followed close behind, whereupon several tiny hands suddenly grabbed them by their hair and roughly pulled them to the ground. Face first in the dirt, Tara tried to struggle but was pinned by several little arms. Dwarfish faces peered into his but he noticed their tiny eyes didn't glow as their larger counterparts did. They addressed each other in a language he didn't understand as the two young captives were dragged off through the darkness.

Lela was kicking and screaming but was just as helpless as Tara was. They were dumped into a side chamber where several other small tunnels snaked off into the murky shadows; the only exception was that this particular one had a large glowing crystal mounted in its center. They dropped Tara to the floor first, and he rushed over to assist his companion as she was released. The little men scurried out of his way like scared insects and peered fearfully from behind small boulders at their tall guests. Lela brushed herself off while snarling at them in contempt.

"We won't hurt you," Tara offered solemnly, while attempting to sign the gesture with a motion of his hands as Gree had taught him.

One of the little creatures approached him cautiously but kept a respectable distance. The small imp spoke in a series of jabbers the boy could not understand in the slightest. The dwarf tried to sign back with little more effect. All Tara could make out was the word '*Nest.*'

He presumed they were inquiring as to why they were in the cavern of eggs, what he might consider a nest for the giant beast. The boy tried to sign back in several different ways that they were trying to escape the large shadowmen, and he could only hope that these two races weren't close allies. More of the little creatures were brave enough to come out of hiding since the two children didn't seem particularly dangerous, though they kept a discreet distance from Lela and her vicious glare.

Tara did his best to correspond by drawing figures in the sand, and even duplicated some of the writings Gree had attempted to teach him before. The little people, however, were far more interested in the pictures the boy drew and they indicated that the large shadowmen were definitely not friendly to their kind. A few of the doll-men came up to touch his skin, which by now had turned quite pale from lack of sunshine.

The language barrier was much more apparent here, though after several attempts they could get the basic structure of their meaning across. Their native language was complex, almost musical, not like the rough mumblings or whispered grunts of the larger shadowmen.

The small creatures were far friendlier than their previous captors, since only Gree had been kind enough to associate with them, and here, Tara had repaid his kindness by socking him in the mouth. The boy admitted that he felt a little bad about that.

The children were starving and the friendly residence brought them a variety of raw fungus and portions of some mysterious uncooked meat. Tara didn't know what kind of animal it came from but anything was better than trying to dine with a live fish wiggling on your plate. He set the flesh on the tip of his sword and cooked it near the orange stones. With their hunger satisfied, there was still the problem of finding their way out of this place.

Lela had no wish to converse with their new hosts, but she did press Tara to ask them where they were. He learned that the bird creature was captured when it was very young, and as it grew older it became trapped in that chamber and was eventually domesticated as it had become dependent on the small men to keep it fed.

The miniature men revealed the large beast laid hundreds of eggs at once, and did so several times each cycle, although a few of the hatched chicks managed to escape to the surface. Tara was encouraged by this news and inquired how the young chicks had done so. The little men responded by informing the boy that he didn't want to go up to the surface, for the land burned during the day and froze during the night, they warned; and down here, where the climate always stayed the same, was the only logical place to exist. Noting their fruitless attempts to offer caution, Tara remembered the problems he had before trying to convince Gree that the surface world was much different than what his people had imagined. He thought it ironic that when he was a small boy, he had been taught that nothing could possibly live underground in the choking darkness of caves or beyond the veil of night.

He could see how these creatures would be virtually blinded and their eyesight would be greatly diminished in the bright daylight. The Dwarf's stature was certainly not built for speed and he imagined they could be easily picked off by several types of predators on the surface, but Tara had a problem understanding just why there was such an absolute lack of knowledge about these various Shadow Tribes among his own race?

Tara had heard whimsical myths about goblin-like creatures when he was a small child but from what he knew now, those stories were grossly flawed. Perhaps whatever childhood tales had been recited in the past had been so entirely unbelievable that they were eventually dismissed as imaginative fairy tales and legends of lore, which were merely told to excited young children as entertainment. The fact was, the only surface-dwellers he was aware of who had ever made it down this far to discover these strange tribes of men who lived in shadow, had found themselves hopelessly trapped. Tara worried this might become their fate as well.

The diminutive creatures they had encountered before

were merely simple workers, and the youngsters met many more of their commune as they were led through several connecting underground villages. The whole complex was made of huge stone buildings, they were very old and obviously made for someone of Tara's size. Among them were familiar carved stone faces and other broken statues with the features of surface men. He discovered these buildings had been here for countless cycles, built by ancient surface-dwellers long ago.

Within the buildings, Tara could barely read the ancient petroglyphs from the faded etchings and tarnished paint, and he was astonished by the story they revealed. Long ago, surface-dwellers constructed multiple underground villages and massive cities. It was a sensible project, since there were numerous natural caverns to build within. These subterranean territories protected them from the heat of the sun during the high noon seasons of the day, and equally so, from the freezing cold during the long season of nightfall that spread across the lands.

They occasionally emigrated as Tara's clan and others had in this era, but their people would also frequently take refuge during nightfall in underground shelters like these, supplied with stocks of provisions gathered during the season of light. They managed to provide additional heat for the underground cities from the natural hot springs using ingenious piping and waterworks they had forged. The inhabitants learned to raise subterranean crops and domestic herds to feed themselves through the long winter of night, and they enjoyed great celebrations when each season of sunrise arrived at the approach of dawn. Here and there, Tara found the familiar symbol for his firefruit. The ancient inhabitants had at one time grown vast groves of these particular plants for use as cooking fuel and they utilized the white crystals as a source of light to push back the darkness.

It was an entirely different civilization of their people's past that moved freely between shadow and light, and for a time it seemed as though their culture had flourished. Tara tried to imagine for a moment what it would be like not to be forced to chase the sun across the land, to be able to settle down and call one place home. It was a concept he had never known.

These strange little people thrived within this deep subterranean city. The small inhabitants said that when they came upon this place they were delighted to find a whole town already constructed for them by ancient giants, even though it was more than a little oversized for their stature.

The boy tried to deduce where the pygmy men had originated, but could only speculate that at one point in their past that certain villagers either became trapped underground, or, by will, they had chosen to remain submerged from the lands above for whatever reason or circumstance; and thus, had evolved into the various clans of Shadowmen. These races of cave dwellers had physically changed by acclimating to their surroundings, and were now obviously better adapted to subterranean life. Through the generations, these little people had evolved this way to use the restricted tunnels and scarce quantities of food available to them. He then reflected on the giant warriors of the Forest Tribes and considered this analogy of their affected growth and size must certainly have some basis.

The elaborate plumbing system that once existed was now in ruins and many parts of the city had been destroyed from cave-ins, but the majority of these forgotten ruins were in relatively fair condition. Its new occupants had kept the usable dwellings in good repair and had blocked off access to the geysers long ago, since infrequent disasters had struck and caused the boiling waters to flood the ancient city in their recent past.

Their drinking water came from a tiny underground spring that had once been tapped for use in the central fountains, although its original piping had long since been destroyed. Their tiny hosts pointed towards a passage to the surface where the young bird creatures they called 'earaks,' had been seen to escape. The two children looked up longingly and felt their hearts leap when they saw a pinhole of sunshine far above them in the cavern ceiling piercing through like an arrow of light.

Spurred with new hope, they inquired how the old inhabitants used to gain entrance from above. Guided to this area, they were disappointed to find the massive stairway entry was now completely blocked; apparently, the ceiling had fully collapsed and the majestic staircase was now nothing but a solid wall of boulders and rubble that clogged the passage.

Perhaps a major cave-in had permanently trapped the inhabitants here long ago, and they had been forced to learn to survive underground, or perish. Tara couldn't justify this reasoning if he could imagine himself in a similar situation; especially so if there was the manpower at hand, unless there was an unforeseen reason they hadn't dug their way out.

These dwarfs did not possess the black stone tools that the other shadowmen used, and had no knowledge where they could possibly acquire them. Even if he had a pick and spade made from that miracle obsidian, Tara guessed it would take nearly a whole cycle for just the two of them to try and dig a way out through the collapsed stairwell. Their only chance was to reach that point of light in the ceiling far above but they couldn't imagine how to reach it. The walls were far too smooth, and the domed ceiling looming far above seemed impossibly out of reach.

Lela let go of Tara's hand and ran toward a tall building at the center of the ruins, where she rushed up its stairways to the top of the highest roof. She clambered over stonework and statues to reach that lone shaft of sunlight piercing through the darkness from the cavern ceiling. Once there, Lela tenderly held the ray of light in the cup of her hands, feeling its warmth, and with a glint of sorrow in her gentle eyes, she began to cry.

Chapter 11

They spent much time sitting in the dusty barren courtyard, staring up at the unreachable point of light far above. Though the ancient city was bustling with life, the friendly cave dwellers could not raise the spirits of their two young guests. Tara finally suggested an idea.

"If only the walls were made of mud, we could carve our own steps into them as we had before," he noted.

"But they're not," Lela muttered, "even so, the opening above is nearly in the middle of the ceiling, and there's no way to reach it from the walls even if we could manage to climb that high," she responded to the reality of their predicament.

"Perhaps we don't have to reach that section. If the sunlight is coming through there, then the surface can't be too far above from the outer walls either," he added. Lela just flashed him a disconcerting look.

"If the area between the cavern ceiling and the ground above was so thin," she retorted, "then it likely would have caved in by now as it had over the main stairway," she deduced with her own logic as she turned away in frustration, "and it doesn't even matter, since we don't have those stone chisels, anyhow."

Tara wandered off, desperately inquiring about the obsidian stone tools with the smaller inhabitants; hoping perhaps that the city builders had left some behind but they had no such luck. He wished he had swiped one before they fled the tall shadowmen in their apparent escape to nowhere.

Tara, being the diplomat of the pair, had managed to

squeeze some information out of his tiny hosts. One of the dwarf men knew where he could acquire some of the stone tools he had been so inquisitive about, but was pressed to keep it a secret. Tara traded his only pair of blue warming stones for this information but apparently, would have to relinquish more valuable trinkets if he wanted to draft the little swindler as a guide.

From him, the boy learned that far beyond these ancient ruins, there were a cluster of forbidden tunnels that the small inhabitants had sealed off long ago. Past the geysers, there was a hive of shadowmen where one could acquire these tools he desired, if one were quick enough. Tara did not want to face the shadowmen again, but obtaining those particular tools was their only chance of escaping this place. He talked Lela out of a turquoise bracelet that she had swiped during the tavern brawl when they last gambled in Hagda. The boy presented this valued prize to his little friend as barter for his services.

He was told to leave Lela behind as not to arise too much suspicion, and they departed for their secret expedition. Tara had to tie his robe around his waist for the passages they ventured were so small that he was forced to crawl on his hands and knees, and squeeze through as best he could.

They used a handy light crystal, which was much more convenient and was certainly a lot safer than using a smoking torch in the confines of the cramped tunnels. Upon reaching the barrier his guide had spoken of, Tara was directed to break away the thin plaster that sealed the entrance by using his silver sword. His guide took a moment to warn him of a deadly type of fungus as he pointed out the bright red plants. He informed him that if they were disturbed, even by the presence of something from a short distance, that its toxic spores would release and could kill him in an instant.

Tara thought it was pointless to do so, but they quietly tiptoed past these strange plants with great care. In afterthought, he wasn't about to doubt the word of a local. They passed through winding tunnels that shot steaming plumes of humid air where the walls themselves were covered with a spectrum of colorful minerals, while Tara had to help his small apprentice cross the wide pits therein.

Beyond this hurdle was the hive of a large tribe of shadowmen Tara was not familiar with. These tall creatures bore stripes of white paint among their limbs and acted much more barbaric as they barked at one another in deep guttural tones. Beyond the group, he could view the layout of their village from their tiny perch high above the cavern floor.

They resided in small huts, unlike Gree's clan who preferred to build their dwellings upon tall stilts. In the center of the group of structures sat a large glowing boulder that they danced around and threw some sort of ash upon, which created a plume of sparks when it made contact with the massive orange-colored crystal. Tara knew how dangerous those rocks were and wondered why they were acting so recklessly around it. They also spotted many more savages climbing down the cavern walls towards the ceremonial gathering below.

He would have to go alone from here on, for even bribing his small guide with a fortune in jewelry would not help the little man if he were captured, for he would stand little chance of defending himself against such large assailants. Tara's tiny companion described how these savages killed enemy clans without mercy, bound up their bodies and laid them out as fertilizer for their fungus crops, which would be a horrible fate indeed.

Tara was careful as he climbed down the wall in the dim light provided by the radiant lichen growing about the cavern walls. He didn't want to leave his light crystal behind; however, its brilliance would have been too conspicuous for the stealth that was required at this moment. The deep shadows made him anxious and the boy could imagine the dark-skinned creatures hopping out of every murky crevasse he crossed.

He dared to jump inside one of the clay huts located a fair distance from gathered revelry; the interior of it reeked of stale mold and sour fish. He ransacked the hovel the best he could in the consuming darkness, but was optimistic about what his fingers had found as he brought the object into the brighter light of the doorway. His eyes were rewarded by the sight of a small ebony chisel that glinted in the flare of the distant sparks.

He quickly shoved the chisel into his boot and was momentarily weighing the thought of searching another hut for a larger blade, but had a change of heart for fear of getting caught. Tara quietly made his way back to the edge of the wall but was startled as one of the striped barbarians jumped out of the darkness in front of him, its glowing eyes wide with shock. The painted tribesman grunted quizzically, staring the boy up and down, wondering what kind of creature he was.

Tara could only take the initiative. He swung fiercely at it with his shikar and swiftly took off on a sprint in the opposite direction. The thing jumped back, startled at the attack and hooted a cry of alarm; and Tara began to wish he had just gutted the beast when he had the chance, which would have been the prudent thing to do. There was a dimly lit tunnel at the far end of the huts that he made for, not knowing where he was headed, but at this point he didn't have any other choice available to him. A dozen of the lanky beasts sprang erratically around him, hooting in a language far removed from his own.

The boy spun around, making a desperate swing with his silver sword, but these creatures were agile enough to slip from reach. Glancing behind him as he plunged into the adjacent cavern, he ran headlong into a grove of fungus and fell flat onto his face.

As he lay momentarily stunned in the soft broken moss, he peered upon a hideous sight, the broken roots of the fungus revealed rotted flesh and bones beneath the clotted surface. Tara scrambled to his feet in disgust. He looked around in fright while his imagination could make out every odd hump or form in the moldy soil as that of a corpse hidden beneath its surface. Tara stumbled through the soft dirt underfoot, trying to make his escape. The natives, however, had become more agitated with their unwelcome guest and had rallied in numbers, and were following close behind.

He hurried forward, making his way to a portal of dim light, which was his only friend against the drowning darkness. Before Tara noticed what was ahead, he had stumbled headfirst into a natural tunnel made of the orange parchstone. He froze momentarily in shock, bracing himself upright with his sword.

One of the excited savages jumped in behind him. Tara turned at that moment to see the barbarian's unprotected foot strike the surface of the crystal floor. The creature's entire leg instantly shriveled to an ashen white. It gave a hideous scream of terror as its fragile leg snapped and he fell to the ground in a heap. Its entire body slowly turned a ghastly white as wisps of vapor escaped from the holes where its eyes had once been.

The band of wild shadowmen stopped short at the small opening to gawk at the horrible fate of their comrade. Instead of following, they jabbered and threw loose stones at their trespasser. Unable to dodge the rocks, Tara became as still as a statue and stared down at his feet. By luck, he had landed on a part of rocky soil, but he was still in contact with the softly glowing orange stone where his leather boot was now smoking from beneath its sole.

The boy had to chance it, for his boots were the only thing that kept him from becoming instantly fried. He imagined that perhaps it was the rapid conduction of moisture from the skin that created such horrific results as he had witnessed; he would certainly have to experiment with that thought at some point, that is, if he survived this little jaunt. Tara made it down through the tunnel until it extended to a patch of hardened soil and into a massive cavern beyond. He looked back with a mixture of forlorn and relief, for his would-be captors were left far behind, but he knew he would never find his way back to the pygmy village on his own.

The cavern air was moist and a thick odor of salt filled his nostrils. Unfortunately, there were no luminescent lichen growing within this section of the cavern, but Tara happened upon a loose shard of quartz he found and was amazed to discover that it glowed brightly when he placed the crystal splinter in contact with the orange parchstone.

At the edge of the cavern, he saw what appeared to be a smooth and glossy formation. As he approached it closer, the object became somewhat familiar. When the boy walked around it, he could see what appeared to be large black eyes in the odd stone peering back at him. The mass of gray skin rippled and the boy froze in his tracks. This mammoth beast was a type of fish, and he could make out the large fins farther down the great length of its body. A catch this size could feed a whole village for half a cycle, but it was apparently helpless as it lay beached upon the dry ground.

Tara was mildly surprised to see that the thing was somehow still alive since he thought that fish needed water to breathe, or at least he was sure they did. Tara didn't dare approach it closer, for if the hulking beast twitched or moved a fin, it would certainly crush him under its tremendous weight. Recovering from his initial shock, he noticed the lapping of water coming from near its tail. He hoped there wasn't another way the wild shadowmen could enter this cavern but speculated if they had another passage to this room, then they would have certainly carved up this mountainous beast to feast upon.

Tara made his way to the waters edge behind the mammoth creature, where the dim glow of his light revealed several more waterborne creatures strewn along a vast subterranean beach as if they had somehow all crawled up upon the shore on their own. Many of the smaller fish were already dead, although a few still struggled and flopped about. With fascination, he discovered several other types of creatures with eerily transparent bodies. Tara jabbed one smaller fish with his sword and took it back with him to the crystal tunnel, where he cooked a dismal meal for himself while contemplating his bleak situation.

Tara briefly wondered how all those fish had gotten

themselves upon the dry shore. The larger creatures were both terrifying, yet curious to study. Some had long snake-like bodies with ghastly wide jaws set with hundreds of needle-sharp teeth, while others had long tentacles and a multitude of eyes that lurched about. The monstrosities twitched about in an eerie silence but seemed harmless enough out of the water, so Tara dared a few more closer inspections for the sake of curiosity.

For a brief moment he thought he could hear a distant waterfall, like the roaring of a huge river, it was then that he began to notice that the shoreline was creeping upon him. Suddenly, the vast underground lake began to bubble up violently, raising the water level as it surged. The tide started to approach with more enthusiasm and Tara began to wonder with a note of worry how high it would rise. He had failed to notice the long pale stain of a waterline decorating the rock walls far overhead, and it revealed his fate if he did not find a way out of this chamber, and soon.

Tara saw many holes that he might be able to reach but only when the water level would allow him to float that high, but who knew how long he would have to tread water or what grim creature would gobble him up from beneath the surface as he bobbed about helplessly. Tara scurried up and down the cavern rim, searching desperately for some form of escape.

The sound of rushing water was echoing off distant walls and his head felt uncomfortably funny as the pressure rose. The water was beginning to lap up to the edge of the cavern walls as Tara was forced to higher ground. A few of the water-beasts made a play for him as they again found freedom in their own element.

Tara was forced to wade through the waist-high

tidewaters all the way back to the entrance from which he had arrived, where he dreaded having to face the savage shadowmen, let alone the hazardous passage through the burning crystals. He looked at the bottom of his leather boots; the treated hide was baked halfway through, its thick leather soles, now hard and brittle. The boy contemplated using shingles of rock as stepping-stones through the passage, but it was far too late to go searching for loose stones in the rising water or he risk being dragged under by the grisly creatures that dwelled within.

The water level rose and trapped him inside the tunnel as he backed away, though he was a bit curious to see what would happen when the water reached the translucent orange stones. As it touched the first edge of parchstone, a thick cloud of steam arose. The boy could see that he would shortly be cooked alive by the boiling water if he lingered for long within this cramped tunnel, let alone if he was swept off his feet and fell upon the glowing rocks. He shuddered at the thought.

Tara sheathed his shikar in his belt and ran as fast as he could, hoping that the crazed shadowmen weren't still waiting for him on the other side of the passage with their sharp grinning teeth, but to his relief, they were nowhere in sight. He nearly fell as he reached the end of the deadly tunnel. He saw yet another pile of dried bones at the edge, for apparently, one of them had tried laying down a sheet of fungus to walk upon but their attempted stunt to create a bridge of moss had failed dismally.

Tara could see small puffs of smoke erupting from the soles of his shoes as he hastily grabbed for the lip at the end of the tunnel and launched himself outside.

He searched around and crept behind a mound of tall

fungus, a moldy skull peered sideways at him from beneath its fleshy canopy. It had been a long while since he had first escaped from these barbarians who had become bored waiting at the tunnel entrance, and failed to find the fatal foolishness of their deceased clansmen to be entertainment enough to keep their attention.

Tara ditched the crystal shard that lit his way, for he didn't want to draw any undue attention. He could feel that the soles of his boots were now quite thin and flaking apart. He fancied that perhaps with the use of some sort of protective leather gloves, small hand size parchstone's could be used as a particularly nasty weapon against a foe.

He crept the long way around, spotting a few of the savages who momentarily entered the fungus garden, then abruptly departed. Steam began to hiss out of the burrow he had just escaped from, and the air became warmer as clouds of vapor rose to the ceiling. Whether the fungus plants here grew larger because of the frequent bursts of warm steam or from the flesh of the dead as fertilizer, he could only guess. Tara's only hope was to make it up the far wall to the exit in time before he was sighted, but he didn't fancy his chances.

He braved a quick glance around the corner and saw that the savages were back to their ritual dancing around the massive parchstone at the center of their hive. Tara was beginning to wish he had brought along his last firefruit to use now, for these shadowmen certainly would have never seen an actual blazing fire and its light would have blinded them and allowed a clear avenue to escape.

Tara used a trick Lela had taught him and tossed a stone far away from his position as a distraction. To his initial disappointment, however, there was no reaction from the shadow-creatures as they were occupied chanting and dancing around the glowing boulder to the point that Tara's little diversion went completely unnoticed. He tried again, this time his aim was off and Tara accidentally hit one of the savages square in the head.

"Oops, now I did it," the boy grumbled to himself as he quickly slunk behind the corner. However, instead of investigating where the stone was thrown from, the begrudged savage took to assaulting the fellow behind him, who was of course, not at fault. A full-scale brawl broke out, first two, then three, escalating to eight, which quickly jumped to over a dozen of the brutes who scuffled among themselves using fists and clubs to express their temper. Evidently, their tribe was very prone to violence.

Tara made his way behind the small huts and past a clump of colossal stalagmites to the far wall, and began to climb back up to the narrow hole where he had first entered. The savages were still fighting furiously and only a few others were actually making any attempt to end the quarrel. Tara almost lost his grip and nearly fell to his death when his little companion's head suddenly popped out of the burrow mere inches above him. His pygmy friend just smiled at him with a creepy grin. Tara was struggling through the little hole when he heard another outcry from below. Quickly glancing back, he could tell they had both been spotted. The shadowmen began to give chase as they swarmed up the wall to reach the invader of their sanctuary.

His small guide ran through the snaking tunnels with ease, while Tara scraped his hands and knees in the fumbled rush. Only a few of the savages, who were of smaller stature, could wiggle through the constrictive portal in pursuit, while the others began violently chipping away at the entry in an attempt to make the passage wider. Their whoops and cries echoed through the narrow tunnels as Tara and his escort fled in haste.

Tara tried as best he could to catch up with his guide who held their only source of light, running far ahead through the twisting passages. He caught up to him in the tunnels as his little friend was forced to wait for Tara to help him across the wide pit therein. The savage shadowmen easily caught up with the pair, and they barely evaded the reach of their spidery arms as they leapt across the chasm.

Running ahead, Tara's small guide glanced back at him once, flashing what appeared to be a mixed look of worry and anguish; then hurried on. A little confused by this, Tara understood his despair in the frozen moment that followed. He jumped out into a small room and past a clump of the deadly red fungus; his boots almost brushing them as he passed. Without pause, Tara dove into the adjacent tunnel behind the dwarf, taking but a moment to glance behind him and paused in shock as to what he saw.

The unfortunate savages trailing behind, ran headlong into the fluorescent red plants as they burst violently into a lethal cloud of white glistening spores that filled the chamber. In that dreadful instant, something horrible happened to the creatures. The the foremost victim stood for a moment as if frozen, just staring towards Tara; and within seconds, his whole body plumped out and shattered into dozens of splinters as if his body had turned to glass. The same process began to happen to his companion who entered the smoky chamber behind him.

Tara was grabbed from behind by his little friend, who was stronger than he looked, and anxiously tugged him farther down the tunnel as the dense cloud of spores began encroaching upon them rapidly. Tara squeezed himself through another small orifice and was quickly shoved out of the way as the miniature creature rolled a large stone over the exit. He then did something that took Tara quite off guard. The little man vomited up a stream of thick pasty goo, which he spat over the seams of the rock that quickly solidified to seal the tunnel beyond. At the sight of this, Tara started to feel a little queasy and felt like he was going to be sick. He turned away, for the stench of the sticky vomit was dreadful.

They finally made their way back to the stone village, and the little man reached high to pat Tara on the rump, much like one would pat someone on the back for a job well done. He tried hard to smile back at the little man who had globs of yellow puke still caked upon his chin. Lela stared in shock at the sight of him as Tara found his way back to the courtyard.

"What in the name of all that is holy have you been up to?" she inquired, still gawking; for Tara was covered from head to toe in dust, bits of fungus, and wide streaks of grime covering his soiled tunic. By intention, Tara had not told her about his planned excursion with his little guide so as not to worry her. With a sigh, he wearily pulled out the obsidian chisel from his boot and handed it to her.

"I'm famished, is there anything decent to eat around here?" he groused as he slumped to the floor in a tired heap with his hands placed lazily behind his head. His gaze rose to meet Lela's dumbfounded expression as she was left speechless at what he had placed in her palm.

Chapter 12

Tara managed to tend to his various cuts and scrapes, and tried to explain his little misadventure through mouthfuls of roasted earak meat.

"I knew you would get mad if I went without you, but the little man and I couldn't tell anyone," he tried to explain. She remained angry for quite some time and divulging the dangers of his encounters only made things worse. When Tara regained his strength, they tried their new tool on the cavern wall. The obsidian chisel cut the stone much better than a metal one by far, but they found it was difficult to manage without a proper hammer. They borrowed a few tools from the local dwarfish members, but these were far too small for their needs.

The dwarfs even tried to help them with this task, but they weren't used to mining through rock. Most of their time was kept busy eking out a living by tending to their bird flocks and fungus gardens. Tara had begun his digging at the top of the tallest structure he could find built against the cavern wall but he had only managed to carve a mere half-dozen fragile steps after a great amount of effort. Lela came up to see how he was doing.

"*Ugh*! I've been working on this for nearly two beads," he motioned, "but without a proper hammer..." Tara tossed away the borrowed miniature hammer in disgust, "I can't go much faster. Besides, I've gotten as high as I can reach and I can't chisel away rock like this while also trying to hold onto these shallow steps!" he finished complaining in frustration. Lela turned away a moment in silent thought and addressed his concerns.

"We will just have to think of something else," she
stated flatly. A sinking feeling of hopelessness returned
to haunt them as the two children sat on top of the
building looking up the sheer wall and the lone beam of
daylight that taunted them.

Tara remembered seeing a few shadowmen who bore
crude obsidian blades that were fashioned much like his
silver shikar. These they used with much more efficiency
as it left one hand free to grasp ledges with, but he wasn't
about to go back to their hive to look for another tool.
Stonecutting was beyond his set of skills. Lela stood and
pulled Tara up to his feet with a sense of newfound hope.

"Let's get something to eat and you can tell me more
about that lagoon with the monstrous fish," she suggested
while pulling Tara down the stairway back to the cavern
floor. The boy gladly dropped his tools to take a moment
of rest.

After hearing Tara's story again in detail, she began to
ask him many questions. Lela was trying to determine
why the tide would sink and rise so dramatically in that
cavern when the underground rivers they had seen before
never reacted in that fashion. She concluded that the
saltwater and the large fish meant that they were close to
a nearby sea, and the water level of that subterranean
pool must have some connection to the pressure caused
by the nearby geysers.

Tara didn't understand anything about air pressure, but
she halfway managed to explain why his ears hurt when
the water level began to rise. Tara tried to convince her
that there was no way they could get back to the solitary
lake; besides the fact of not knowing just how long those
deadly red spore plants could remain dangerous after
they had burst. He vividly described what he had

witnessed, and did not wish to risk meeting a similar fate.

After spending a useless amount of time debating over their situation, they had failed to come to a suitable resolution. If inclined, they could manage to survive within these ruins with their small hosts, but living like this was very uncomfortable for them and it was also notably difficult with that shaft of sunlight beckoning to them from above. Both of them finally agreed that they would have to take their chances back out in the geyser canyons, giant slugs and all.

They collected as many supplies as they could carry and paid for these with another trinket from Lela's stash of loot, and offered a few last good-byes to the pygmy tribe. A few of their little hosts guided them back through the tunnel and hurried them safely through the room of the giant earak, which was busy tending to several dozen of its young that had recently hatched. Tara still found it amazing that its tiny offspring could grow to such an enormous size.

The young couple withdrew back into the passage near the ancient ruins, and their small guides bade them a final farewell as the little creatures promptly sealed up the doorway behind them. He had warned Lela about their uncouth method of doing this, so she hastily removed herself from the scene before they started.

This time, the two companions were well equipped with a few of the light crystals from the pygmy village and felt much safer with them, even though the illumination from the lichen here was at a fair level to see by. It was now Tara who wanted to take this opportunity and explore the small tower they had found earlier. Lela was adamant that they should just forget about it, since there was no way across the steaming water but Tara tempted her curiosity with enticing hints of long-forgotten treasures, for he knew her weakness.

After much thought, he guided her to the raised walkway and began to chip at the small dike that retained the water within, which had once acted as a simple bricked enclosure that eventually filled with stagnant mineral water. The obsidian chisel made short work of the wall itself. He simply made a small hole in it near the ground to allow the steaming water to escape.

It took a while for the pool to drain far enough for the original walkway to emerge that was now covered with a thick sludge of mineral deposits. Tara was astounded that the door to the tower had been made of real wood, which he would have expected to have fully rotted away by now but instead, had petrified into stone. His precious black chisel came in quite handy for this task. The petrified wood was actually much harder to chip away than he had first expected. It cracked down the center and Tara busted it in half with a stout kick of his boot, and they squeezed their way inside.

Whatever had been stored on the ground level had turned to a kind of indiscernible blackened mush. At the far end of the room there was a treacherously thin stairway without rail or handholds, that ran up in a spiral along the wall. The second floor was also windowless, where they found an empty chamber with mauve-red walls. Upon the floor lay an exquisitely woven carpet showing faint embroideries of farmers and fields and other examples of surface life shown under a blazing sun.

This delicate carpet disintegrated to dust when they walked upon it, each step they took left a telltale footprint of their passage on the fragile fabric. At the far wall, they found another stairway that led up to the third floor chamber door; but now all that remained was the skeleton of thin splinters that had once been a thick wooden hatch. Upon the third floor, they found a stockpile of old decayed weapons, some so rusted through as to be unrecognizable. It was here that Lela found a silver necklace symbolizing some long-forgotten deity hanging upon the wall, this bauble she swiftly acquired for her personal collection of stolen goods.

In a small decayed box, Tara found what looked to be amber glow stones, but the source of their mysterious light was now long dead. Upon the walls was a mural depicting a fully armored warrior equipped for battle, while drawn along the border of the ceiling were silhouettes of strange creatures they could not identify.

A ladder made of rusted steel led up to the fourth and final floor, but its rungs crumbled beneath the slightest weight. There was something of brilliant gold that glinted through the portal overhead, attached to the domed ceiling in the room above.

Lela became unreasonably thrilled to find such an item, as the gilded artifact beckoned to her. The decayed wooden boxes and piles of rust would not take any abuse without disintegrating to dust, and they risked cutting themselves on the old rusted metal remains of the ladder. Tara remembered his chisel and tried carving thin steps up along the wall. He attempted to cut along the side as high as he could reach, but Lela shoved him aside impatiently and climbed halfway up the wall by nimbly grasping the protruding stones. Tara shook his head and chuckled because she was still far short of the ledge.

Lela found a crack in the rock and shoved her belt knife inside, cramming it in up to the hilt. Tara looked on in amazement as she used the embedded handle of the dagger as a handhold and used it to reach farther to the ledge above.

"What's up there?" Tara shouted to her. He heard a little bit of scuffling from above, but her head finally popped out of the shadows to peer down at him.

"Nothing but rags and something that looks to be a bed," she answered. He then saw her climb among the stone beams of the ceiling to reach the glittering object hanging there. It made a soft ringing noise as she broke off the rusted chains holding it in place.

"What is that?" he inquired curiously. Tara wasn't about to try scaling up there as foolhardily as she had.

"It looks like a golden bell." she cried back with glee, as she polished off the dust layered upon it.

Lela clambered back down but couldn't manage to pull her knife loose from the wall again where it had been inserted. As Lela coveted her golden prize, Tara tried to chip away the stone around the stuck knife, but it was difficult to hold onto the wall with one hand and have any leverage for such a chore that was nearly at the tip of his reach. After a short time, he jumped back down to the ground while feeling a little disappointed.

"I can't seem to get it out; it's jammed in there pretty good," Tara conceded in defeat.

"It's okay, I really don't need it. Besides, I got this!" she smiled, holding up the small golden bell in her hands. Strange, he thought, that such a bell in a tower must have been used as either an alarm or a signal, but why make one so small and out of precious gold for that matter? As they left the room, Tara glanced back at his old trusty knife that his father had given him, now hopelessly embedded in the crumbling wall. 'I sure hope it was a good trade,' he thought to himself while trotting back down the stairway.

They made their way out of the haunted tower and back towards the pathway beyond when Tara noticed that a collection of sludge was already beginning to clog up the hole he had carved at the edge of the pool, as it started to refill once again. While making their way into the geyser canyons, Tara examined the strange bell. He had never seen a design of its like before. It was shaped like an oblong fruit with several small decorative holes bored into its sides. When he tapped it with his crystal, it rung with a pleasant airy chime. He had to admit that it was certainly worth more than his old knife.

Most of the rough edges of the canyon were easy to climb; this jagged subterranean landscape was likely created by a violent quake long ago. Progress was slow, but their crystal lamps came in handy in areas of the depths where it was too warm for the glowing fungus to survive. As they entered one narrow chamber they began to notice broken pieces of skeletons and piles of bones scattered about the cavern floor, most of which looked to be like young earak remains. Lela also noted some strange looking cone-shaped shells lying about the ground that were the same texture and color as the surrounding stone.

There were many holes bored into the ground, not deep ones, but smooth pockets penetrating only a hands length into the dirt floor. What had created them was a mystery. Tara kicked around at the earak remains, at first he thought they died there from exposure to the heat or lack of food but soon noticed that every single bone had been thoroughly separated from its corpse.

Tara called to his companion, who was again sitting on a rock and playing with her golden chime and she got up to approach him. Lela had just gotten to her feet and began to brush off the soil from her dress when something slammed into the floor behind her. Lela jumped back and screeched in alarm. In that split second after he had called her, Tara saw something large fall from the ceiling, landing where she had just been sitting a moment before.

She was very lucky, he thought for a frigid moment, for a stalactite had broken loose from the ceiling and crashed to the ground where she had sat. Lela was frozen in shock as he stepped over to her. The stone spike was as nearly as tall as she, and it balanced there, impaled into the ground.

Lela approached this broken stone with curiosity, and as she was about to touch its rim, she froze in fear. To her horror, long spidery legs began to emerge from the cone of the stalactite. She wanted to scream but the sound of it caught in her throat. Tara unsheathed his shikar with one hand and grabbed her shoulder with the other. In a distressing moment, they realized that the stalactite was not a natural stone, but a hollow shell like the smaller ones Lela had examined earlier; with the exception that that those husks were empty of its occupants.

A dozen long black legs emerged from the top of the shell, which was attached to a bubbly pustule-like skin surrounding a mass of jagged beaks. Several black eyestalks peered out of the thick casing to scrutinized them and the ground surrounding it. The entire shell began to wobble back and forth as the creature flexed unseen muscles to shift itself free of the soil where it was embedded. They both yelped in alarm as another shell missed them by a hair, lancing into the ground just inches from where they stood.

They both jumped back and glanced up towards the ceiling. Holding their lights higher, they could see dozens of stalactites moving across the roof of the cavern among the dancing shadows. Those things were aiming for them! The first critter had managed to topple over, releasing its shell from the floor. Now upright, it scuttled towards them. Tara struck at its shell fiercely but his blade only glanced off of its stony armor with a shower of sparks and caused the cone to waver unsteadily as its tiny beaks snapped at him in fury.

As they retreated, the predators above realized that their prey was now aware of them and they began to rain from the ceiling like a hail of stone spears. Tara led their way while dodging the shower of stone spikes that pelted the floor around them. In their haste, they bolted through narrow breaches in the rock and over several steaming ponds they would not have otherwise dared to cross. Their panic led them far away from the shelled creatures and they didn't stop until they reached an outcropping of bedrock, under which they hid.

"It seems those things can't move very fast," Tara panted while trying to catch his breath.

"They probably don't need to," Lela breathed as she flopped to the ground in exhaustion, "they probably just skewer their prey from above and consume their crushed remains." They both quickly acquired a new habit of survival in this strange subterranean world, and learned an important rule to always look above them.

The flow of air picked up dramatically in the enormous cavern they had stumbled into, where the force of the warm drafts was considerably stronger. Trying to fight the howling winds, Lela nearly lost all of her veils as the ardent gales caught them and ripped them from her dress.

One piece of sheer material was nabbed from her grasp and blown farther into the cavern, where it danced in the wind until it disappeared into a tiny speck in the distance.

A thick fog formed from the violent geysers, where angry clouds gathered on the ceiling, swirling in furious circles.   Here the lichen, growing well in the rich moisture and heat, brightly lit the interior of the cavern. Climbing over small gaps to adjacent canyons, they could not escape these subterranean storms.   Alternate routes only proved to be more precarious than the last.

Showers of bitter water briefly pelted them when errant gusts of wind shifted their way.   Fierce cyclones of moist air momentarily breathed into existence, only to quickly die away.   Passages over a strange smelling gas escaped through vents with a piercing roar.   The air was hard to breathe and they both felt dizzy to the point of collapse, though luckily, these effects soon wore off after departing the chamber.

They both lay there resting, trying to clear their heads when Tara saw something quite strange as though from a lucid dream.   From beyond the jets of thick gas approached a ghostly form.   Walking on three legs, one on each side of its round body, the large form strode along in a circular motion.   Upon its spherical body were large plates of scales, three short arms, and where its head should have been, sat a large mouth.   The sickly gray thing had no eyes as far as Tara could tell.

'What a strange hallucination,' he thought to himself as he lingered in the foul gas, but Lela's panting screams told him otherwise.

The creature came directly for them, flexing its tiny hands in repetition.   One stubby forearm grabbed Tara with near crushing strength.   The intoxicating gas had caused the boy's reactions to slow dramatically. He felt strangely groggy and almost began to laugh at the strange beast that seemed unreal, but the increasing pain of his arm told him otherwise.

This close, Tara could see the beast had a huge mouth filled with large, flat teeth. Lela hurled the largest stone she could find at the creature, barely missing her companion that was held in its grip. Oddly enough, the thrown rock simply stuck to the side of its monstrous body, whereupon, one of its loose stubby claws peeled the stone away and flung it down its gullet.

'If it likes rocks, why bother eating me,' Tara thought to himself; still groggy from the intoxicating gas. Tara turned his shikar towards his assailant and was dismayed as he thrust the entire length of the blade into the beast, without effect, as the horrid creature failed to react to the mortal blow. He pulled the blade upward to tear a hole in its flesh, but as the blade passed through it, no mark of any wound was left in its wake. 'Oh ...I am so dead,' Tara told himself while impaired from the effects of the poisoned air.

The creature secured his arm and was dragging the boy farther back into the gaseous chamber, and Tara could feel his mind slipping away as he was enveloped by the toxic gas. He choked violently on the acrid air filling his lungs. Lela didn't know what to do, she had seen him pierce the monster through with his sword and it seemed like there was no way of harming the creature.

She absently fumbled for her knife, suddenly realizing she had left it behind in the tower. All she had at her disposal was her treasured bell and the obsidian chisel Tara had dropped from his belt when the creature had seized him. Lela wasn't about to let her friend be dragged off into that creature's lair without a fight! She didn't have time to think about the consequences, since she knew Tara wouldn't last more than a moment in the gas-filled alcove if the creature dragged him inside.

Lela picked up the black chisel, contemplating for a brief moment that the small tool was grossly inadequate as a weapon, and ran up to plunge it into the side of striding beast just as it reached the edge of the grotto.

She was shocked to hear the walking boulder howl in pain at the minor injury she had inflicted upon it. Lela released her grip upon the small chisel and watched in astonishment as it slowly sunk deeper into the flesh of the creature on its own accord. The plump beast immediately dropped Tara to the ground, where he rolled about the floor in a delirious state.

The creature spun about frantically, then its fat stubby legs gave way underneath it and they felt the shock as its heavy body crashed to the ground. The place where she had stabbed it with the obsidian chisel began to sink in upon itself, turning the entire wound black as it spread across the creatures body. It was fascinating, yet horrible to watch. Within moments, the monstrosity was nothing more than a bubbling pile of flesh and oozing intestines that inflated and popped.

Using all her strength, she dragged Tara far away from the horrible scene to an outcropping where they could find fresh air. Tara only mumbled incoherently, and it was a long while before he regained his senses.

Chapter 13

"Ow, my arm hurts!" Tara groaned in pain when he finally awoke. Cradling his bruised shoulder, he tried to sit up only to discover that he didn't have the strength. Lela ran over to him as he began to stir, bringing him fresh water and dried bird meat from their rations.

"I would have bandaged it up for you, but I didn't know how badly you were injured," she responded gently. Tara's head bobbed as he peered around in a daze.

"Uh, wha …what happened?" he stuttered, trying to remember recent events.

"That giant rock eater from the poisonous cave attacked you, but I killed it," Lela confessed.

"Whaa …*you* killed it by yourself?" he blurted as his mouth dropped open in disbelief.

"Yes," her eyes wandering off, "you could even say that I rescued you," she smirked.

Tara tried to smile back, but shifted his shoulder at that moment and only managed a painful wince in response. Peeking under his tunic, he found his whole arm was now thoroughly bruised. Lela ripped away the outer layer of her dress to make a sling for his injured arm; the monstrosity had done some real damage to him and it would take some time to heal.

They made their way back to the grisly scene where several tiny crab-like insects scurried away from making a meal of the dead creature as the couple approached. Tara removed his silver shikar from the pile of guts and goo, but no amount of searching through the puddle of its bowels revealed their prized chisel.

Slitting open one of the organ sacks, they discovered hunks of raw ore along with many small clumps of gold and gemstones. Tara wouldn't dare touch them, but Lela couldn't help herself.

"It looks like it could digest rocks, but not gems," she stated, cleaning off the hunks of ore and precious stones with a spare rag. Tara shook his head.

"If it eats rocks, then why did it bother with me?" he answered with a mild sense of deja vu creeping into his head when he repeated the words.

"Maybe it thought you might taste better," she giggled lightly. Tara just frowned back in response, there was always the possibility that the bizarre creature was simply defending its territory.

Mystified as to why they couldn't find the obsidian chisel among the remains, Lela tried to explain to him what she had witnessed. They left shortly thereafter because the billowing toxic gas in the vicinity of its lair was starting to affect them again. After spending much time scouting the area they could not locate a single safe route to the canyons below, nor through the boiling geysers and wind funnels. Lela mentioned she had seen some passageways within the gas-filled cave from whence the creature had emerged, but Tara knew they wouldn't last more than a moment in there.

"We just have to hold our breath," she suggested.

"Are you nuts, for how long could we do that? We would suffocate to death. That's probably why that *thing* drags its victims in there, so they can't fight back when it gobbles them up!" Tara replied.

"Look, if you don't want to give it a try, I'll dash in there and take a quick look around and be out before you know it," Lela offered to sate his doubts.

"And you are just going to hold your breath while you run around?" he scoffed at her for being so irrational.

"Yes ...I can do it," she stated with earnest.

After a short but heated exchange, Lela ran off into the mist without his approval. She was going to do what she pleased whether he liked it or not. She took a few deep breaths while Tara stood at the mouth of the chamber behind her, yelling at her about how reckless this was while she explored the hazy alcove beyond.

She was gone longer than he expected, and Tara started to get worried while feeling the weight of guilt for letting her go in there alone. She suddenly reappeared, running out through the pale clouds of gas, panting heavily, her wet hair clinging to her face. Shaking his head with disapproval, he helped her over to an area with some fresh air.

"I saw many tunnels, a lot of dead ends but there's one that leads somewhere, I think," she gasped. Tara began to scold her again but she cut him off, pointing to an area around the bend of the cavern, "See how the ground descends in this alcove ...the passage I saw may lead past the geyser cyclones," she stated, showing Tara the area.

He was still not convinced, for if the tunnel she indicated was yet another dead end, he was certain that they would both pass out long before they could turn around and make their way back out again to safety. Lela handed Tara their water skin and told him to drink. She guzzled down as much of it herself as she could, and dumped out the rest on the ground. He stood there, startled at her strange behavior.

"What are you doing, we're going to need that!" he barked.

"We've got another bag of water, besides we need this

just now," she answered bluntly as she patted the empty canteen. Lela took many deep breaths and blew up the empty water skin until it reached its maximum expansion, then she promptly sealed the nozzle tightly.

Still thinking Lela was acting strangely, Tara gathered their provisions and made ready to rush through the passage, with a measure of doubt clouding his mind, much like the cloudy chamber he gazed upon. They both took a deep breath and darted for the corridor, Tara following her lead. The thick noxious gas plumed out around them, but the monster's lair was devoid of any bones from its previous victims. The tunnel walls were certainly not natural, it almost seemed like there were large bite marks taken out of them.

They had made it a good ways down the corridor but were still surrounded by the putrid gas, and Tara's lungs were about to burst. Lela stopped him for a second and Tara wondered how he could argue with her while holding his breath.

"Whm mu doomg?" he hummed out to her while keeping his lips sealed.

Lela let her breath go and took a gulp of air out of the inflated canteen, then handed it to Tara and motioned for him to do the same. They continued their progress down the tunnel and tried that exercise twice more while they were still on the run. This time though, they used up the last of the spare air they had within the wineskin.

The tunnel branched off into smaller trails, but Lela kept them running down the main passage. Tara could no longer hold his breath and started panting while taking in gulps of the bad air that made him feel instantly dizzy.

'This is it!' he thought to himself, and somehow found their current situation a little funny from the effects of the gas. They were both bracing each other as they stumbled along, their muscles becoming weaker by the step. Tara felt unreasonably exhausted and just wanted to lie down and sleep. At that moment, it seemed like a sensible option but Lela dragged him onward.

Stepping forward through the thick mist, the ground suddenly gave way beneath them. Hidden by the gaseous fog, they failed to notice the sudden slope in the floor. All too late to catch themselves, they were swept off their feet and slid down into a narrow tunnel; helpless to slow their drop on the slippery stone. Drugged as they were by the noxious gas, their muscles refused to obey as they tried to slow their descent.

One moment they were airborne, the next they slammed backside first into a floor of thick ice. Tara's rear now hurt even more than his shoulder did. He mumbled deliriously until the effects of the poisonous mist wore off. He crawled over and woke up Lela, who had grazed her head upon the hard ice. She finally came too and uttered an odd giggle as she tried to stand.

"Are we out?" she asked hopefully, her eyes still rolling in her head. Tara looked around to an ice-filled chamber; the air was so chilly here he could see his own breath in front of him.

"Yes, we're out of the strange vapor and into a real fix!" Tara picked up the light crystal they had dropped and took a look around their icy cell, "Why did you keep running down that central tunnel?" he questioned Lela as she rubbed her sore head to answer.

"I was watching the flow of the mist on the ceiling, I figured it would lead to a way out of there; but I didn't see the hole in the floor," she grumbled as she held her sore head.

"Neither did I," Tara confessed. It was nobodies fault, and there was no use fighting about it.

The floor was very slippery here and several columns of thick ice decorated the room. At least it refracted their dim light well enough for them to see by. Tara found a thin sheet of ice and tried to chop his way through the wall with his sword. The ice cracked away and fell into a room far below, but what he saw there was disheartening.

There was a young earak, at least of some age because it had grown to match their height; it struggled there with its large clawed feet embedded within the icy floor.

"How did it manage that?" he whispered to himself as Lela came over to take a look through the small window in the ice.

The earak squawked halfheartedly, visibly tired from its struggles to free itself. Lela thought she could see discolored clumps embedded within the floor below, but she couldn't tell what they were. Tara looked around at their icy cage surrounding them and found a large puddle of chilly water at one end of the room. Curious about this, he watched as it slowly drained away. There was a faint gurgling noise as the water level diminished.

Through the window, Lela thought she could see snowflakes falling into the cavern below and called over to Tara. They watched as the white flakes swarmed around the helpless bird, which landed on it momentarily until the earak began to beat its stubby wings in desperation, trying to shake them off as the animal began to squall even louder.

"Those are insects," Tara stated in surprise.

The snow flies harassed the helpless bird as it flapped about, though it couldn't escape as it was hopelessly pinned by the ice. The parasitic flies were biting and sucking out a few drops of blood wherever they landed on its body and could get through its thin layer of feathers. The flies retreated momentarily, and Tara was now beginning to wish he hadn't chopped a convenient hole in the wall for them to come through.

Shortly thereafter, a distinct sound of rushing water could be heard echoing through the chamber. From the area where Tara had found the pool seeping from their cell, water flowed into the room below, surrounding the poor animal. In an instant, the few inches of cold water froze and solidified into hard ice around its limbs, and the bird was embedded even deeper into the floor. Once again the excess water in the room drained away with a similar faint gurgle to another level farther below. Lela began to look worried.

"That's water from the geysers above. How long before it fills this room again?" Tara asked with foreboding.

If icy water came pouring into their cage, there would be nowhere safe for them to climb. The chute they had fallen from was far above their reach and Tara could not do much damage to the thick ice with his sword. Looking below, the earak was beginning to weaken. Now rooted deeper than before, they could tell the animal was slowly freezing to death, while the swarm of flies were taking full advantage of its fresh blood before the layers of ice entirely froze over their trapped meal.

Horrified by this realization, Lela placed her light crystal against the transparent floor beneath them. Below their feet, deep within the ice, she could make out huddled figures within frozen clouds of blood encasing them. She could only gaze at Tara with a look of despair. An odd buzzing sound and a needle-sharp pain behind his ear got his immediate attention.

"Ouch!" Tara hollered as he slapped his neck, he saw a spot of blood on his hand, and a crushed snow fly fell to his feet, "Look at the size of this thing!" Tara exclaimed, rubbing his neck and nudging the dead bug with the toe of his boot while its sharp stinger scraped the ice.

The buzzing became louder and Tara gazed bleakly at the hole in the barrier he had created. A mass of snow flies began to flow through the small opening into their chamber. Lela dashed about the room screaming, but there was nowhere to run. Beating off such a large swarm was hopeless and they suffered many bites. Then, just as suddenly, the pale flies quickly withdrew.

They watched as the insects swarmed high to the ceiling above, followed by a loud gurgling noise. There was nowhere to escape as freezing water began gushing in through hidden channels in the ice. Lela tried to block the spouts with strips of clothing from her skirt, but most of the outlets were far above her reach. At first, the water was only ankle-deep, and then the few inches that covered the floor began to quickly freeze.

There was a slight slope to the room and they tried to huddle against the higher ground near the far wall. The ice water swirled freely about the chamber for a moment then began to drain out the far end of their frigid cage. They had to continually pry their feet up to keep them from freezing to the floor. With the water receding, the snow flies began to descend upon them once again. They just weren't getting a break!

Lela tried to avoid the stinging flies, but she was only wearing sandals and her feet were now turning quite blue with frost. Her thin shoes began to stick to the ice even though she tried to adjust her position, but eventually her feet turned numb. She slipped and ripped the back of her dress open on a sharp shard of ice that protruded from the wall. Her hidden back pouch tore open, spilling its valuable contents across the glassy floor.

Being the heaviest of all her items, the golden bell slid farthest across the room and into the shallow puddle of water draining from the chamber. Tara tried to urge her to forget about the jewelry as she vainly struggled to gather them, only to drop everything she had grasped when she tried to swat away the huge flies.

"This is hopeless," Tara shouted in distress. They were either going to freeze to death or be eaten alive by these albino insects, or likely, both.

He swung his sword in vain at the insects, though it was wasted effort as his blows passed harmlessly through the swarm. He saw the bell in the puddle, intending to use the larger object as a means to swat the flies, he reached out with his shikar and pulled the chime out of the cold water with the tip of the sword as it slid all the way down the blade on its ring to the handle of his weapon. It rung dolefully as it hit the hilt, but something amazing happened when it was struck.

All of the snow flies surrounding him shattered like frail crystal. More bugs came in, biting him on the arms and back. Tara rattled his blade again, and the chime rung louder this time. He watched in amazement as more of the insects surrounding him burst into white shards. Tara gave a spirited "Ah-hah!" as he dried off the glittering bell with his robes, and rang it once again.

This time the knell resounded throughout the room, causing their vision to shift. Lela fell on her rear in shock and nearly every snow fly surrounding them shattered into tiny pieces. Tara rang it again as loud as he could to kill off the rest of the insects, and succeeded in that measure as the entire room reverberated again.

His vision warped as before, as if he was looking through a pool of water whose stillness had been broken by the dropping of a stone, and at its center was the golden chime as the air itself rippled. However, this time huge icicles started to break off and drop from the ceiling above, busting into splinters around them.

"Is that bell doing this?" Lela tried to scream above the sound of crashing ice around them.

"It killed off that swarm," he shouted back over the noise of the cracking ice. Hugging herself and shivering terribly, Lela motioned for him to hold the bell near the opposite wall towards the window they had cut earlier.

Tara rang the bell again, lightly this time. A section of the wall wavered from the high-pitched tune and crumbled away, he tried again to make the hole bigger. To their utter shock, the ground cracked beneath their feet and suddenly gave way. Powerless to stop their fall, they dropped out of the hole and slid into the cavern below. The walls of ice gave them nothing to grasp onto as they hurdled down the frozen slide.

Ahead of them lay a large glacial pool and Tara squinted his eyes against the shock of being dunked headlong into the icy pond. Lela slid in splashing behind him. Luckily he had strapped his sword onto his forearm or he would have certainly dropped it, but it had suddenly become a weighty burden when he tried to swim to the surface with only one free arm to paddle with.

He abruptly noticed that Lela had not come to the surface. Dunking beneath the waterline once more, he saw her still body sinking below into the depths as he released his grip on the shikar and shook it free from his arm. He plunged deeper into the clear frigid water to grab her. He had never actually been submerged in water this deep before, and it pained his wounded arm. The numbing cold made his mind ever more alert, even as his body started to defy his will while his limbs began to succumb to the cold.

He saw bright shafts of light illuminating an underwater passage ahead and struggled to pull Lela's body in that direction. In the depths beneath them, Tara saw their light crystal sinking far below and what looked like something very large and snake-like chasing the glowing shard as it descended into the cold abyss.

He barely made it through the underwater tunnel and climbed to the surface, gasping for air. The glaring light nearly blinded him as he pulled Lela to the shore. When he dropped her to the ground she began to cough up small amounts of water. The shock of the freezing water had stopped her breathing momentarily, otherwise, her lungs would have filled and she would have surely drowned.

She lay there shivering, not even being able to speak as Tara desperately tried to wake her. He knew they had to get warm, and fast. He unfastened the last firefruit he had strapped to his back and the flint from his pocket that he grasped as a blessing for not having lost in the frigid pool. He knew the torch would light despite its dunking and snuggled beside Lela as he warmed his hands against the blazing pod while its dancing flames roared to life.

For the first time, he got the chance to scan the new landscape around them. The hissing of natural geysers could be heard from distant tunnels and he felt a warm breeze upon his face. It was the blinding light from above that made his heart leap, even as he squinted from the sight of it. As his eyes adjusted, a crack of bright blue sky streamed in from a huge rift in the ceiling, shining sunlight among a cluster of ancient ruins and green plants in a wide cavern the size of a small valley.

He carried Lela over into the sunlight. They had been stuck so long down here that he had almost forgotten the warmth of sunshine. He gathered some dried wood from the surrounding brush and trees in the grotto and made a proper fire. Their food rations were lost and their remaining water skin was punctured, but he found a few scarce handfuls of wild berries to fill his stomach.

Lela finally stirred and huddled near the welcome fire. She could only gaze around in wonder when she saw the sky, and the sight of it lifted her spirits. Tara made a hunting sling from a strip of cloth, and with a few stones he managed to kill a few small birds for them to eat. Above them, he saw a flock of birds sheltered in nests made of dried mud along the edge of the fissure.

At first, their skin began to burn in the direct sunlight, and they teased one another, for they could now see just how pale they had turned. Tara's shoulder still ached terribly and Lela constantly sniffled and sneezed, and was visibly ill from her dunking in the freezing glacial waters. They were a pitiful sight indeed.

They stayed in the immediate area of the sunlit ruins for a spell. Tara went to chase birds, and with the selection of brush and plants around he was able to make a basket trap that was much easier than slinging stones. They were very pleased to see that the sunlight fell in nearly vertically from the rift above. This meant that they must have been traveling in the direction of the sun, rather than closer to nightfall as they had feared.

It was Tara's turn to be the hunter-gatherer and to take care of his companion. Lela was still recovering as she laid in the shade of a small tree, protecting her now ghostly white complexion, but with all his running about, Tara's own hide had begun to peel and blister from his sudden exposure to the direct sunlight. The boy frequently took dips in the brisk pond to cool his sunburn, always wary of the huge creature he had seen before that lurked in its frosty waters.

It took some time before Lela began to feel better, for she had become quite ill, but the hot meals seemed to help as he nursed her back to health. She was still a little weak, but as soon as the bump on her head fully healed she was her old self again.

"You dropped your sword back in the spring?" she blared at Tara when he finally admitted to losing it.

"I couldn't very well swim with it; besides, you kind of needed my help at the moment when you sank like a stone," he marked in his defense.

"And the gold bell ...and all my jewelry?" she moaned sadly while searching through her ripped pouch.

"It's either back in that ice cave or it sunk to the bottom of the shaft I presume," he granted, but Lela got up and strode over to look down into the depths of the pond.

"I can probably dive down there and get them," she speculated, but Tara grabbed her arm to stop her from being foolish enough to dive in after the jewels.

"You were unconscious, Lela. You've just healed and that icy cavern is far beyond reach, besides, that pool is far deeper than you could possibly imagine," he spouted in caution as she just grumbled wistfully with a defeated pout stamped upon her face, "And there's something alive down there, one of those water serpents or something of the sort; whatever it was, it was big!" Tara exclaimed as Lela took a jerked step backward away from the waters edge at this alarming news.

As they recounted what had happened with the strange golden bell, Lela mentioned a particular woman that once traveled with her clan many bands ago who was a talented stage performer, one with a voice so trained and could sing at such a high pitch that she could shatter fine glass with her voice.

Of all her jewelry and gems she had lost, Lela mourned the loss of that peculiar golden bell the most.   Tara quietly grieved for his lost sword but he couldn't bring himself to feel guilty about it in the least, for saving Lela was far more precious to him than any gilded weapon. This insight caught him off guard, realizing he was deeply in love with this little gypsy girl, but he didn't dare tell her.

Chapter 14

The children so desperately wanted to reach the surface but were convinced that practicing a little discretion from this point forward was best. It looked like a fairly easy climb out of the sparse few crevasses that presented themselves; but without any weapons, they didn't want to chance running into trouble with the local wildlife they might encounter along the way. Tara doubted that there would be any Shadowmen within the vicinity of this exposed cavern since their eyes couldn't stand the direct sunlight, and there were no telltale niches decorating the cavern walls.

Along the fringe of the cavern where they had first entered were a couple of heated geysers on the opposite side from the cool spring. A few peculiar hollows they discovered there led into the gloomy darkness beyond, but they weren't about to explore these. In the middle of the cavern were many plants and small trees which hadn't grown very tall within the limited sunlight that the rift in the ceiling would allow. The ruins themselves were ancient structures resembling a temple of some sort. Cut within the cave walls were the same designs and craftsmanship they had seen before on the towering cliffs back in the hidden valley.

There was no sign of life here besides the chirping of birds and a few small lizard-creatures that scuttled away from underfoot and amongst the stones. They searched cautiously among the deserted ruins, not wishing to be caught off guard by any new creatures or circumstances that could thwart their plans this close to the surface.

There were many ancient artifacts they were accustomed to finding, such as old discarded items left abandoned by this long-forgotten civilization. Very few petroglyphs had survived the ravages of time and weather, and little else was found.

Unlike the ruins in the jungle valley, they found access to every room in the upper floors here. Someone had gone to great lengths to carve intricate reliefs upon the walls, depicting dancing animals, unknown gods, and warrior heroes with great detail. The rooms were so elaborate and cleverly designed that they almost hated to leave, and the young lovers were fond of the idea of having their own private palace.

The couple finally discovered a safe passage to the ledge above; a crumbling stone staircase, greatly eroded by time but clear enough for them to climb. Lela meticulously combed the area for treasure in every room they entered, though nothing that glittered met her scrutinizing gaze. In the last room they crossed, she noticed a tall vase that had survived intact sitting hidden within a dark corner.

She convinced Tara to try and drag it into the sunlight so that she may look down into the narrow neck of the urn, however, the bottom broke when he tried to lift it. A bundle of onyx chisels of different lengths tumbled to the floor at their feet. Lela displayed a moment of complete joy, for having lost all of her precious treasure, she wasn't about to let these rare artifacts slip through her fingers, knowing just how valuable they were.

She hastily wrapped the shafts along within their decaying cloth with a strip of her own dress, which left her shapely legs nearly bare at this point. They had little trouble climbing the staircase to the surface above but found it to be precarious footing, while they ascended as many of the cracked steps broke away beneath their feet and tumble to the crumbled landing far below. They shaded their eyes as they breached the top of the stone stairway, for the whole surface seemed to be ablaze and they had become unaccustomed to the bright light. Upon the surface, a hot wind greeted them as they found themselves in the middle of an arid desert, though Tara swore that he could smell the faint scent of salt lingering in the air. They stood there in the blazing sun, wondering where they could be.

The young couple stumbled towards the distant roar of water; as imprudent as it was, water still meant life, and they were at a severe disadvantage in this unforgiving heat since they no longer had their canteens. They were no more than a few dozen steps from the cavern exit when Tara turned to survey their surroundings, but he could hardly see the cleft they had emerged from as it was well camouflaged by the surrounding terrain.

This region was so flat and littered with large broken stones that anyone passing within a few hundred feet could easily miss the massive rift that hid their secret glen beneath the harsh desert surface. Tara tried to keep his bearings on the cavern mouth as they continued onward, but quickly lost the entrance amongst the rough landscape as the distance grew. They had walked until they were exhausted. Their skin was burning and they both started to feel the pangs of hunger when they stumbled upon a vast ocean shore. Beyond the haze over the water they saw another stretch of tall cliffs beckoning in the unreachable distance.

Tara closed his eyes and tried to remember the maps his father had showed him in the past, and drew various lines in the sand trying to recall what he could from memory. He knew there were only three oceans that spanned the region and deduced that they must either be on the north or south fork of the Eon Sea, but he wasn't sure which. He remembered his father's rigid teachings, for Torg had tried to prepare him well as he had hoped one day his son would lead their tribe. It was of crucial importance to know which fork this actually was, for the center of it only led to the deserted city of Olan that once was a thriving hub for travelers and trade.

The desolate metropolis of Olan resided upon a narrow bridge of land that led directly to the empire of Silistra, but a long time ago a portion of the land sank into the waters, leaving only a broken string of mountain tops now known as the Veil Islands. With transit by water shunned as it was, no one was willing to travel the great distance inland to Olan, just to make another trip around the vast shoreline to the main trails; and thus, the ancient city was left abandoned.

They slept there on the beach at a safe distance from the lapping water, tired and hungry while halfheartedly making shade as they could with the long grass growing there in the soft white sand. It wasn't long after awakening that Tara scouted ahead and came across a well-beaten path. Farther down this road they stumbled across an etching on a large milestone indicating the symbol for the city of Te-Na. Finally, they had nearly reached civilization! They tried to jump for joy but were simply too exhausted to do so. The painted figures showed that the city was only two beads away ...but that was measured by mounted travel, not by foot.

Tara was certain that his clan would have left Hagda by now, but didn't know what route their caravan would have taken on their continued journey. Lela didn't seem to care much about finding her tribe ever again, being the kind of single-minded outcast she was; but Tara truly missed his father's presence.

Their only hope would be to find a roadside water well or natural spring along the way. By now, Lela's feet were becoming very sore and Tara's brittle boots started to fall apart. Tara had lived a lifetime under the bright sun, but after dwelling in the cool shadows of darkness for these past several bands, the children had become accustomed to the cool subterranean world and now the sunlight itself seemed like it was melting his skin away. He couldn't remember ever being so hot!

Their pace had slowed and the two companions were starting to feel very weary for lack of shade and fresh water. They were scouting for another spot to make camp along the roadside when Lela noticed a low cloud of dust billowing in the distance, which was the possible sign of an approaching caravan. They began to wave and flail their arms in display of their anticipation, but realized that they were still too far away to be seen through the wavering heat rising from the desert floor. After waiting for their approach, it appeared that a huge party of travelers was advancing in their direction.

Their salvation approached at a steady pace on the dusty road to Te-Na. They sat there in the hot sun, trying to stay awake from the lack of food and complete exhaustion as the party slowly advanced. As the convoy grew closer, they could now see that it comprised of mostly men, Tara could not recognize their tribe for they presented no emblems or flags. He found it unusual that they rode on great oversized wagons pulled by huge rorns. Some rode smaller beasts, and they had nearly a dozen large unsaddled rorns tethered to a line. There was also a large caged cart in the middle of the procession, which appeared to be packed full of skins and gear.

Their foremost scout wore a black turban with a length of its cloth enshrouding his face, protecting him from the dusty plains. At his side, he wore a large gem-encrusted blade that seemed to be outrageously large for a knife, which was secured to his belt by a braid of thick gray hair that looked strangely out of place. The man raised his hand to halt the troupe following behind.

"What do we have here?" he leered down at the pair of weary youths. Tara tried to relate who they were, where they've been and what they had been through, all in one parched breath; but it came out sounding like gibberish. Lela finally interrupted his rant while trying to manage a slightly fatigued, but discreet smile.

"Good Sir, we are lost and need some supplies," she implored while removing the ruby headpiece she still wore from her tangled hair and handed it to the mounted rider, "we will pay for some food and water and a lift to the next city," she finished wearily, trying not to appear too desperate and retaining her sense of dignity, despite their ragged appearance.

The man held up the soiled gemstone to the sunlight, its sparkling red reflection dancing across his eyes, while a wide malicious grin grew upon the bandit's face behind his darkened veil.

* * *

Their new hosts provided quantities of spiced meats and bread along with a few skins of water in trade, half of which almost disappeared immediately as the two children were ravenous. Gorging their appetite almost to the point of making themselves sick, the young couple laid down in the back of one of the enormous carts laden with thick rugs and furs. Lela tried to cuddle with her little man.

"Ooo, don't touch me, I think I'm gonna throw up," Tara groaned as Lela tried to hug him. Having tasted normal food for the first time in what seemed like eons, they had severely overeaten. Lela felt about as sick as Tara looked, so she laid there in the sunlight beside him, wheezing for air.

Strangely, they noticed that there were only a sparse few women in this ragged caravan, and no one bothered to speak with them. Their clothes were ragged and torn, which made them look like a pair of poor street urchins, and realized they would have to get new clothes when they finally reached the city of Te-Na. One of the men continued to bother them after they finished their meal.

"What do you have there?" he pressed with a leering grin at Lela while patting the bundle of black chisels near her side. Lela's mind worked fast to fabricate a response.

"Oh, those are just lumps of coal," she tried to think of another lie, but left it at that. The nosy cuss ogled the bundle for a moment, only to turn away in disinterest while grumbling under his breath as he was oblivious to their true value.

After getting some much needed rest, when they awoke, Tara could tell they were nearing the city, its massive bronze walls and broad towers could be seen in the distance. A great arc of deep green forests and vast stretch of mountains lay upon the horizon beyond. Looking around, the boy noticed what appeared to be a barath strung along far in the rear, but it was hard to see over the clouds of dust the carts kicked up.

"Lela," Tara asked, turning to her, "does any of this

seem familiar to you?" he inquired with suspicion.

"What do you mean?" Lela returned with a shrug. They bounced along as the sound of the creaky wooden wheels rolled underfoot.

"I mean these oversized carts, and their mounts are the size you would expect forest giants to be using," he whispered.

"They probably just traded for them somewhere," she trailed off, unconcerned.

"Yeah, but rorns are *very* expensive, especially full-grown adults, and they have all those extra mounts tethered together trailing in the rear ...and they also seem to have a vast overabundance of food, and I thought I saw a barath strung far in the rear," the boy remarked.

"So?" she whispered back, making a slight effort to glance behind them.

"Well, the fact alone that rorns travel much faster than baraths in this type of terrain. Besides, its well known that the two breeds don't get along very well together, and I also thought I saw a basket saddle strapped to it, and only Plains Tribes use such gear!" he finished. Lela bit her lip and appeared a trifle upset at his query.

"Look, right now we're in no position to make trouble for ourselves," she huffed as she grabbed him by the shoulders, "we made it out Tara, out of those terrible caves. I thought we would never see sunlight again, trapped underground in that world of shadows!" After a few troubled moments, she finally calmed down, "When we get to the city, then we'll get cleaned up," making an exaggerated gesture with her tattered rags of a dress, "and get some new clothes, *then* we will see what you're so damned worried about."

Long before they reached the city gates; while the

exhausted young couple slept soundly, the bandits were occupying themselves with their possessions as they quietly snooped through their meager belongings. After failing to find anything of interest except for a paltry bundle of black stone sticks to rifle through, the men of the bandit clan had a hurried discussion about their new passengers. A few men thought it best to kill the adolescents outright and throw their bodies into the sea, but a few others debated that it wouldn't be worth the trouble to slit the throats of a couple of street urchins for a scanty bag of coal; and besides, as extra cover for their ruse, it might look good to have a few children on the wagon when they entered the city gates. They certainly looked conspicuous as it was with their oversized carts and extra mounts, but a few kids sitting up front would help add to their disguise.

The bandit tribe had a rough time these past few bands, as it seemed that most of the central roads were flooded with more travelers than usual this cycle and this made their trade of highway robbery significantly more risky, as many caravans they spotted recently had banded together into large groups for protection as they journeyed between each of the major settlements.

For many bands they had been dragging along a small herd of adult rorns they had seized from the forest giants, which were useless for them to ride merely because of their immense size. But the creatures where worth a significant amount in trade, so they decided to find a backcountry settlement where they could ditch the animals and their stolen spoils in barter for some smaller mounts and regular-sized wagons. They were used to living on the road, and entering any controlled city was always a gamble, but in their line of work they were used to taking risks.

When they finally arrived at the gates of Te-Na, the city guards halted their caravan for a stretch of time while carefully looking over their gear. Sitting there waiting for the inspection to finish, the young couple noticed that the whole troop had changed their garments while they had slept, and the string of wagons now bore bright yellow flags of some strange tribal crest they didn't recognize. After a lengthy conversation with the central guard, the group was finally let through; though Tara noticed the chieftain handing the guards a few expensive skins and a small bundle of jeweled boxes, which was most likely a bribe to let them pass.

This city was much smaller than Hagda, and the streets here were brown and dirty; even the people here seemed a bit blander. Immediately after they entered, their driver suddenly became quite unfriendly and shooed them off the cart, but Lela made sure to snatch up the food and waterskins they had paid for before departing. Their first priority was to find a craftsman and sell a chisel or two so they could buy some new clothes. They found the locals here to be rather impersonal towards them, but Tara was sure it was because of their squalid appearance.

They finally found an old mason in a market who carved decorative stonework and gargoyles with many half-finished samples laying strewn about his shop. At first, he just thought them both to be a couple of beggars looking for a handout, which was a bit understandable considering their mangy condition. After struggling to get his attention, Tara managed to show the man how invaluable the obsidian chisels would be. Lela smiled at his presentation and mentally gave Tara commendations for his efforts and salesmanship.

The old craftsman was shocked at the ease of carving with the miracle tool, but Lela held out on the price till he nearly gave her all he had saved in valuable trinkets for just a single chisel. It wasn't long before they were back shopping in the marketplace, but finding decent clothes in their size was a task that proved to be more difficult than they had expected. Exploring the small city, they finally discovered a lively backstreet bazaar. Lela traded in her old ragged dress for a forest green gown with soft flowing veils gilded with golden trim. Tara dumped his dusty brown tunic for one in turquoise with intricate gold and silver designs woven along its length, along with a pair of boots and a matching turban.

They washed at a public bathhouse and set out to find any local festivities where they could eat and get some decent rest. Tara promised himself that he would make a visit to the guard post later, to see if by chance his own clan had passed this way. Among the unfriendly crowd, they still caught people staring their way; perhaps because of how comically pale their skin was compared to everyone else, despite their obvious sunburns.

They found a dreary half-filled tent of a fat merchant who was celebrating the wedding of his newest bride, and they paid their entrance for the sparse entertainment and food within. They both looked at each other with slight disappointment as this small gathering was a far cry from the lavish assemblies held in Hagda, where the young couple had first met. Despite the lack of decent entertainment, they spent much time in each other's arms among the pillows, just happy to be safe and alive. There was a little singing and dancing, and the obese groom joked and laughed much too loudly while shamelessly fondling his embarrassed bride.

Everything came to a halt when the town guardsmen came bursting in, causing the fat merchant to abruptly cease his obnoxious laughter. The flustered chap squabbled with these party crasher's for their intrusion but his complaints were quickly silenced, for it appeared the guards were looking for the two youths. Still groggy from the wine they had consumed, Tara and Lela were slow to react as one of the patrolmen approached them.

"Are you the two who sold Glarak, the mason, a chisel of black stone?" he spat at them with an irate expression stamped upon his face. In unison, Tara nodded '*yes*' while Lela shook her head '*no*', as the couple drunkenly responded. "You both are ordered to come with us, the Council of Elders would have a word with you," the irritable guard demanded. Lela gave her companion a worried sideways glance as they were hauled away.

'What kind of trouble have you gotten yourself into this time?' Tara thought to himself.

The Council chamber was far from regal. They were made to wait for an extensive period as the Elder's muffled conversations turned to loud arguments from beyond the heavy bronze door. The soldiers standing guard to the chamber eyed the children with suspicion, making the two youths feel even more uncomfortable than they already were. Finally, the door swung open and they were escorted into the court chamber to a table where the Elders sat. One of the more regal gentlemen bearing a towering hat upon his thin head, spoke first, placing the onyx chisel they had bartered earlier upon the table in front of them.

"Where did you acquire this, children?" the inquisitor demanded. Tara was about to blab, for he had nothing to hide, but Lela covertly elbowed him and stepped forward to answer in his place.

"Why, what have we done wrong? Have we broken any laws?" she stated with an air of self-assurance. All the Elders exchanged baffled looks and mumbled to each other in challenge to the facts at hand.

"Not as yet, but this artifact here is made of a similar stone that was displayed at a special meeting of chiefs in Hagda. We understand you are aware of its special qualities?" the elder inquired.

"Yes, we found them ...in ah, in a discarded vase in the desert," she finished by telling only a half-truth, or half-lie, depending on the way you looked at it.

A guard came in carrying their bag, dumping the contents onto the counter. Their food rations, a few rags enfolding odd shards of crystal, and the incriminating bundle of obsidian chisels. Lela's other valuables were tucked neatly into a secret pouch she had sewn into her new dress, but it was far too small to hold the stone tools. She gave a notable cringe as the items clattered upon the table in front of them. The elders again exchanged looks of astonishment.

"You may not have heard that many settlements have been vandalized and destroyed during nightfall. There has been an ongoing investigation for quite some time but for obvious reasons, all avenues of this dilemma cannot be fully explored. If you have any information on this matter, it is your duty to inform us now," one of the bald councilmen finished. Tara began to blurt out something in response, but Lela raised her voice over his to drown him out.

"We have heard, but we were accidentally separated from our clan and made our way to this city when we happened across some ancient pottery with these stone tools stashed within it, and that is all we know," Lela lied with nary a flinch, which Tara noted, was something she was very good at. While one of the guards leaned over and whispered to the nearest elder, Tara took the opportunity to breathe a question into Lela's ear.

"Why don't you just tell them the truth?" he asked her, completely perplexed.

"Do you want to end up in the Pit?" she growled back, "If we tell them the entire truth, they will think we're insane. Do you really think anyone would actually believe us? Besides, remember the tavern brawl and the incident in the catacombs!" she pressed with a raised eyebrow. She didn't need to fill in the rest for him to the trouble they were facing.

Tara realized she was right. If they got themselves in any kind of trouble and their tribes weren't in the vicinity to save them, then they would be either imprisoned or thrown in the pit to swelter. Besides, they had that charge of theft from the burial vaults in Hagda to worry about; actions with grievous consequences. Tara got nervous and absently began rubbing his wrists with worry. The bearded elder nearest the guard addressed them directly on another matter of concern.

"You both came to this city on a caravan with many other persons of suspicious character, not half a bead ago. How do you explain this?" one of the Elders accused. Lela looked a little nervous as she answered.

"They found us on the trail and gave us a ride here," she responded while Tara nodded beside her. The elder stared at them with a blank face.

"Perhaps we should question the caravan leader," he turned to the guard, "Have him brought in," he ordered with a snap of his fingers and waving the soldier away.

Things were quickly getting out of hand. Tara didn't know how Lela planned to explain how the two of them got all the way from the city of Hagda, to the outskirts of Te-Na on foot. He shook his head in despair and breathed a heavy sigh of resignation. While being detained, the adolescents were given some stale bread and a place to sleep. It was a great deal later when the same soldier came tromping back in with the brigand whom had a very unpleasant expression set upon his face, rattling along as his hands and feet were bound in heavy chains.

Everyone congregated back inside the council chamber. The burly guard dragged in the bandit chieftain, who glared and spat at the children where they stood. The tall guard grabbed his tunic and hauled him back roughly to cease his antics.

"This is the leader of the caravan the children arrived on. By searching their cargo, we discovered that they are nothing but lowlife bandits. Several caches of longbows, poisoned arrows, and stolen merchandise were found in their possession. We only managed to catch this one and confiscated a few of the large wagons they left behind; I'm afraid the other thieves got away," the soldier finished. This did not look good for the young couple.

The elders gave the pair of kids an accusing glance, but the moment was broken when the marauder blared out at them with a seething glare in his eyes.

"My men will come for me, and when they do, you will all choke on your own blood!" the rogue threatened the children who watched helplessly at the turn of events, "...and I will see you two hanging from your entrails for ratting me out," he hissed.

The guard quickly hauled him out of the court chambers

when the bandit started to spout off a series of threats and obscenities. Another city guard came to stand at Tara's side, but not for his protection as the boy had presumed.

"Since you two are children of these bandits, you will be held for trial and punishment," an Elder declared.

Things were not looking good at all, and Tara found himself almost wishing that they were back in the caves; monsters, geysers, shadowmen and all. Lela knew what 'Trial and Punishment' meant in these small towns, especially if you were a bandit. There was a shorter word for it; '*beheading*.'

They were locked in separate cells set side by side in a cold underground chamber. Tara just groaned, and was very angry with Lela for not revealing the entire truth. Even if they were connected to the robbery of the tomb in Hagda, anyone can tell you, it's much better to lose a hand, than your head. In the back of his mind though, he knew she was right about not telling them every little detail; but how could they have known that the caravan that had found them was sired by bandits, and furthermore, how could they convince their captors that they weren't associated with them in the slightest?

Bandit tribes such as these had been indirectly blamed for the destruction to the settlements by popular rumor, and having those accursed black chisels in their possession did not help in the least. Tara was still a little rattled by the violent threats from the bandit chief but either by his hands or by the headsman, the outcome still looked just as grim. After sitting in dank, musty silence for what seemed like an eternity, a gurgled cry broke the air, abruptly ending their stagnant boredom.

The body of a dungeon guard tumbled down the stairwell and sprawled across the floor at the landing;

then came three men, all of them wearing familiar black turbans that veiled their faces. The one posing in the middle removed his mask so they could clearly see his face. Each of the trio held sharp bloodstained shikars. Tara caught a lump in his throat as he stared into their cold eyes. They recognized the marauder with the malicious grin, and the bandit chief stepped over the body of the dead guard to lift the latch to Tara's cell.

"Just here keeping my promise lad," he sneered through his rotted teeth. Lela screamed as the two other men approached and began to open her cage.

A battle cry echoed from the stairwell above and the attention of the three rogues was immediately drawn away. Soldiers poured into the narrow dungeon hall. The first villain was skewered through and screamed like a dying animal. The second could only manage to parry a few blows with his short blade, before he too, had a red hole ripped through his torso. Enraged, the bandit chief stepped forward into the fight in a vain attempt to fend them off, but quickly retreated back into Tara's cell and put a sharp knife to the child's throat.

"Back off or I'll kill the boy!" he demanded, trying to hold the lad still as he struggled. The soldier who had originally arrested the marauder, took a step forward in defiance.

"Go ahead ...save us the trouble, his head is going to roll anyways," the cavalier guard delivered back with a tone of light amusement ringing in his voice.

The nonchalant attitude of the tall guard standing at the entry infuriated the outlaw. He threw the boy aside as he lunged for the soldier. By complete accident, as the boy fell back, Tara's boot caught his assailant's foot in mid-leap. A look of surprise washed across the brigand's face as he fell forward on the soldier's sharp sword poised before him.   The commotion suddenly ended, and the guard wiped clean his bloodied blade on the dead villain's robes.

"I saw you trip him, quick thinking lad," he smirked.

Tara didn't say anything; he figured keeping silent was his best bet on this occasion as the guard slowly strolled over to Tara and helped him to his feet. The boy stood staring with wide eyes at the smeared blood on the guardsman's sword, its polished blade positioned uncomfortably close to him, still not quite sure what the soldier had in mind to do.

"My name is Reem ...Captain Reem," he smiled holding out his free hand, "I could tell by the way that rogue talked about you back in his cell that there must at least be a drop of salty truth to your side of the story," he stopped mid-sentence to motion his men to release the girl in the adjacent cell, "And by the way, my men mentioned how completely derelict you both appeared when you entered the gates. You really must have been picked up along the roadside after all, since you weren't wearing costumes like the others in that band of thieves and cutthroats," Tara only looked at him sideways while the captain explained, "It's an old bandit trick, as they are constantly changing their wardrobe and identities to fool others as they move from place to place. They rarely come to the cities, but they had to trade in their stolen booty some time," he finished as Tara stood up, trying to regain some of his self-dignity.

"I don't understand. If you knew who they were, why did the guards let them into the city in the first place?" the boy asked. Reem answered his valid question in turn.

"We can't just close the gates to everyone we find shady,

we needed time to investigate the matter. The bribes they had offered my guards only managed to raise more suspicion," he chuckled, then quieted down suddenly, gesturing lightly to the corpses littering the cell floor, "Sorry about all this, a few of his men broke in and caught us by surprise, and had managed to release him. They would have gotten away if they hadn't bothered to come back for you two. I guess the fire for revenge burns hot in their blood, even if his anger was misdirected," Reem conceded. As they left the cell, with a kick of disgust, the Captain scooted the body of the bandit leader out of his way.

"Fool!" he jeered at the lifeless corpse as he walked past, his boots splashing in the blood that pooled upon the wet stone floor around them.

The young couple were released from their prison cells and fed better food this time. Although the Elders had failed to do so, Reem apologized for their mistreatment; but there was still the matter of getting their confession. Later, after Lela had faded off to sleep, Tara snuck out of their room and sought out the Captain on his own in an effort to explain their dilemma, while attempting to fill in the missing pieces, which Lela's story had purposefully left out about their epic adventures in the subterranean world. Reem sat quietly as he listened, but graced him with an almost amused expression while Tara recited his long tale.

"Well, it an interesting story but it seems a bit fanciful, don't you think?" Reem stated with a hint of sarcasm in his tone. Tara responded by defending himself.

"If we were able, I could show you the cavern entrance where we had surfaced," the boy stated while looking away for a thoughtful moment, "...although it would be fairly difficult to locate, I couldn't exactly promise that I could find it again," Tara finished, realizing this wasn't helping to support his story much at all.

Reem did have an uncomfortable thought that scratched at the back of his head, that the boy's story was a bit *too elaborate* to be entirely made up. Glowing crystals, lanky creatures that were once men, strange monsters, glowing moss, ancient ruins and whatnot; it was all a little too much to swallow. Then something struck Tara that he had left out. When they were first captured by the shadowmen, he faintly remembered something that Lela did not happen to witness. Tara gave the Captain a stern look, who was taken aback by the boy's sudden change of tone.

"Tell your Elders I wish to speak with them again. I can prove our story and answer the questions they had asked of our tribal chiefs," Tara stated boldly.

Chapter 15

Lela was extremely upset that Tara had been blabbing his mouth off behind her back.

"At least it will confirm our story. And just think, Lela, about what we had discovered, what we experienced was our people's past. Can you imagine how this will change the way we live, the way *everyone* lives?" Tara delivered with earnest. The stubborn girl could not contend with his logic but she didn't want anything to do with what Tara had planned.

At the council meeting, Tara focused on the events of a certain legendary expedition long ago; the famous warriors of Silistra, who had taken that daring journey into the darkness. Reem sat listening quietly in the background as the young boy proceeded to describe his adventures to the Elders. What he portrayed was fairly believable until the part in his narrative where the spidery-limbed 'Shadowmen' had captured them.

Through all the amused whispers and muffled laughter, Tara continued to weave his tale. His mention of the dead heroes and details of their uniforms struck a hushed note among the skeptical crowd. Tara further proved his encounter by sketching out the personal emblem of the legendary expedition's only artist, who was charged with keeping a record of their encounters upon the walls of the palace hall. His tribal symbol was known to but a few of the court scribes, but this soldier's personal mark was certainly not common knowledge.

Tara proposed they should launch an expedition of their own. They had emerged from the caves less than two beads travel from the city, and surely the elders would want to know if he was telling the truth. Tara pleaded with the council that if they were still doubtful, he would trade off all their obsidian tools to pay for this short jaunt should he fail to prove his story true.

The elders accepted this collateral with a droll grin, but Lela passed him an angry glare that made him wince. She later confronted him in private about the deal he had made with the city elders.

"You would give away our fortune? Those stone tools are all we have left from that horrible experience. Of everything we fought and suffered through and you're just going to..." she began to scold him, but Tara cut her off mid-sentence.

"Look, Lela, I will find the grotto. Who knows, maybe you and I are the only ones in recent history to have ever found a way out from that shadow world. It's a part of history about our people that has been long forgotten. It's important ...very important. I have to go back!" he stated with a tinge of righteous sentiment.

Their quarrel gone unresolved, Lela laid down a few harsh words in her rejection and gave him the cold shoulder as he departed from their chambers. She only began to quietly forgive him many beads later while she watched from their high balcony, as Tara rode from the city with Captain Reem and a small escort of soldiers that were assigned to accompany them on his quest.

From the detailed preparations Tara had recommended, they hauled along a score of provisions and other odd equipment the boy had requisitioned for their journey. Rumors about the expedition somehow got out before their departure, and several amused citizens made lewd comments and playful jests towards the party of soldiers as they departed the city gates on their dubious campaign. Many of the young soldiers themselves, had also thought this assignment was just a joke, but they would do anything to relieve their tedium of patrolling the drab city streets. Besides, a short break and some fresh air would do them good, and what possible harm? They would be back in the city within a few beads time, and many of them made light about the outspoken boy trying to find a lost civilization in the middle of a desert. The sheer idea of it seemed ludicrous.

After traveling to the milestone by the great shore, Tara tried to find their old trail off the edge of the Eon Sea, but the blowing winds had swept away their footprints long ago. The boy could only generalize on which path they should take henceforth, so the group of men spanned out across the region into the low rolling hills and the rough broken landscape. Reem rode alongside Tara to address him of their situation.

"Just to let you know, Tara, I was given orders to return back to the city within another three beads time after reaching these outer plains," the Captain stated flatly.

"Only three beads? But ...but I'll need longer than that," Tara cried, "There was no road were we emerged and we didn't have any maps to guide us, and it was hard to tell which direction we had wandered from. It could be just over that rise for all I know," Tara complained, throwing a loose motion towards the horizon, "we need more time than that!" he pouted.

The burly captain merely gazed down towards the passing scrub brush under the hoof pads of his mount.

"Orders are orders young man," he stated again calmly, "...but it might help if we swept the area with scouts; at least we would have a better chance of finding these

mythical ruins of yours within the allotted time," he
offered as a compromise. Tara grudgingly agreed and
they issued the group of men to fan out and comb the
landscape, each keeping within shouting distance of the
other; by doing so, they managed to cover a much greater
area this way.

The first bead passed without incident and they made
camp under the blazing sun. As silly as they thought this
maneuver was, most of the soldiers took advantage of
this short vacation and the liberty to enjoy themselves by
failing to take this tour of duty in any serious regard.
The boy realized that Lela had forewarned him that they
might react this way, so he could not completely
begrudge them.   On their return sweep through the
hostile landscape, one of the men at the outer edge of
their line nearly fell into a chasm, mount and all. He
called to the others, and they regrouped back at the site
they had found.   The men gasped in awe as Reem
inspected the dark gaping hole.

"Looks like we found your cave, although it appears to
be nothing more than a natural formation from an old
dried-up spring. There is no evidence of any man-made
ruins here, I'm afraid," he mentioned, standing up and
moving away from the dark rift. Tara shook his head in
mild disappointment as he stomped around the fissure.

"No, this isn't it," he frowned, his elated hopes were
dashed as he surveyed the scene, "the cavern we climbed
from is much bigger and there was a wide stairway that
allowed passage down from the surface."

"I'm sorry, Tara, but we have to make our way back to
Te-Na after our next camp," Reem announced as one of
the soldiers picked up a loose stone and hurled it down
into the deep hole. In response to this reckless deed, Tara

jumped over and screamed hysterically in his face.

"Don't ever do that!" he panted nervously and stood there in suspense as if he were waiting for something to happen. The surrounding group of men just stared at him peculiarly, thinking the boy had gone loopy or had caught a sudden case of sunstroke.

Reem suggested that they should at least lower someone down on a rope, just to have a look around. Of course, not a single one of the soldiers volunteered, so the captain chose a man at random for the task. Like everyone else in the troop, the poor lad wasn't very fond of the dark ...but orders were orders. Fearing that the sharp edges of protruding rock might gash the rope, the patrol built a solid brace of wooden beams directly over the shaft so they could drop him in vertically.

The scout was given a pair of torches; one to light his way and the other to drop to the bottom to test its depths. The guards gathered around the edge to watch as the man slowly descended, while a few others acted as an anchor while they grunted and heaved at the other end of the line, lowering the soldier below. They tied extension upon extension, as the guide with his pair of flickering torches descended deep into the gloom, until he finally disappeared behind a jutting protrusion of stone. They were nearly at the end of their supply of available rope when a series of sharp tugs and excited yelps echoed from below.

They swiftly pulled the scout back to the surface, where he came up without either torch in hand and clinging to his lifeline with a death-like grip. The soldier's face was pale and he was shivering while complaining about how cold it was down there. They untied him and treated the man for a few wounds, as he had been severely scraped by the jagged edges of the pit during his hasty ascent without any source of light to guide his way.

"It was so dark down there..." the young man muttered in shock and was clearly shaken by his short journey below, "when I reached the bottom, there was what looked to be a columned hallway carved right out of the living stone. I also noticed some broken pottery in the distance, but I couldn't see it very well in the dim light, so I threw one of the torches farther down the hall and there was a horde of these shelled critters with nasty sharp claws that came swarming across the floor. I dropped my other torch just trying to climb out of there before they got to me," he shivered.

All the men looked at one another in disbelief. Reem gave Tara a curt nod, saying a thousand words in that short glance. This recent discovery entitled further investigation, and it would benefit them to bring back some form of evidence for the Council Elders. Tara wasn't too thrilled about having to explore new territory but he had to go along, for he alone was the only one that was most experienced in their group who held any knowledge about the subterranean world below and what they might encounter.

The group of soldiers grumbled as they donned the extra warm robes Tara had insisted for their supply list, which had seemed like a ludicrous waste to carry until this very moment. They secured their packs along with several dozen torches and handheld lamps were lowered down in pairs upon Tara's direction. Half of the men were to stay above, so as to make sure they had a secure anchor to the surface and could provide quick extraction for their comrades if need be.

In the shrouded gloom below, the group of men

shuddered. None of them except for Tara had ever been in such thick darkness as this; for in their society it had always been taught that warmth and light was life, and only the souls of the dead lingered in such consuming darkness. For countless generations, their people had become accustomed to migrating under the sun's path, but here, they were surrounded by utter blackness, and it seemed to suffocate them.

Though Reem was in charge, Tara took the lead. Here was a boy who didn't fear the shadows, and for the moment he was the only one in the group of soldiers with the courage to continue onward. The carved corridor below was fairly tight, where many small crab-like scavengers still scuttled about. These creatures looked familiar to Tara, much like the ones that were feeding on the corpse of the rock-beast Lela had killed. The soldiers, of course, had never seen anything like them before; but the large bugs apparently didn't care much for the light from their torches and quickly scurried away out of sight.

Bits of broken pottery crunched beneath their feet as the party approached a solid stone doorway at the end of the short corridor. There they found a thick granite door with three deep horizontal grooves set deep within its girth, and they tried every way they could think of to open it. Finally realizing they could lift the block of stone; it took four men alone just to raise the heavy slab and they had to hold it in place as the others slipped through underneath into the chamber beyond.

They tried to brace the stone portal with a few wooden sticks of their available torches, but only moments after the last of the men passed through, the frail brace snapped under its tremendous weight and the massive slab slammed shut with a thundering boom. Regrettably, there were no grooves on this side of the portal to allow them to get a grip upon the stone door to lift it once again. Tara seemed casually unconcerned about this, until he finally realized that in their haste and confusion of preparing for their expedition that someone had overlooked a vital item on the supply list, and had apparently forgotten to pack a few of the obsidian chisels for their trek.

The little boy stomped up and down while uttering obscene curses unbefitting for his age, swearing it was likely those damnable Elders who were responsible for refusing to release the relics for the expedition. Now they were trapped, and Tara shook his head in disbelief he had been caught in the same situation again.

The room they now occupied was filled with tall exotic statues that were both half beast and half humanoid. The walls were sparingly decorated with sculptures while snaking vines wove among the walls of the chamber. Tara was familiar with this type of carving, having seen them before in the sculpted cliff ruins. However, this area was all new to him, which didn't inspire confidence for the rest of the men in the group. The strange statues were in nearly pristine condition and the room was fairly clear of debris. Tara, who had learned from experience, kept warily inspecting the ceiling for those living stalactites that had almost cost him his life before.

The large eccentric idols lined the walkway, laying an uncomfortable gaze down upon their passing guests. At the far end, their path abruptly ended at the base of a robust idol, which appeared to be a replica of the bird totem Tara had seen back in the jungle valley.

"Alright, I want two men to stay behind at the stone

gate that closed on us. If any of our men from the surface should come down looking for us and raise that gate, I want you to build a solid brace of stone with whatever you can find to hold it open," Reem ordered.

Two men eagerly volunteered to return to the blocked portal, although, they eventually began to regret their enthusiasm after they realized they would be left behind in the gloom with only a few lamps to befriend them.

Tara walked around behind the bird idol and found what he had half expected to find. Beyond the totem was a narrow tunnel, which abruptly ended at a semicircle alcove showered with hieroglyphs. He shouted to the others and they rushed over to gather beside him. Tara was trying to make out the symbols as Reem and the other men approached.

"Firefruit, six beads, some kind of fungus plant, and an inverted black triangle, and something that looked like a map of a maze," Tara blurted out as he attempted to decipher the images. Reem came up from behind, inspecting the illustrations with his torch.

"What does it mean?" he asked in wonder.

"It's a message," Tara explained, "do you see here..." the boy pointed to some of the ancient hieroglyphs as more of the soldiers crowded into the tight passage to have a look. At that moment, Tara heard the sound of grinding stone from the edges of the floor that made his stomach sink. A vision of the erupting geysers and quakes flashed through his mind as he felt the floor shift ever so slightly. Everyone became still and Tara held his breath as the low grating noise slowly ceased.

Suddenly, the whole room began to slide beneath their feet. The corridor was a trap, and as more men crowded into the tiny alcove, their weight had triggered some hidden mechanism beneath the flooring.

Men shouted while others tried to grasp the slick walls as they began falling over one another. Being at the worst end of it, Tara was nearly crushed in the tumble of bodies. Their torch-wielding comrades burned several other men behind them as the group was ungraciously dropped into a steep chute. Their pain was short-lived as a pool of chill water came up to greet them, and all their torches were suddenly doused ...and then the true terror began. They had been dropped into the most horrible nightmare any man from the surface world could imagine; to be plunged into deep water and surrounded in complete darkness, all the while with something biting bloody chunks out of you.

Beneath the water, Tara's eyes were wide open but he could only see blackness. There were no forgiving shafts of light or glowing lichen to help him get his bearings, and for long moments underwater he noticed how difficult it was to determine which way was up or down without some kind of illumination to guide his way. In a moment of pause, Tara quit struggling and allowed his body to gently float upwards to the surface.

The boy held his breath for what seemed like an eternity, until he finally felt his body reach the surface. He gasped for air and could hear the other men's screams clearly now, many of them were choking and splashing about. Most of them didn't even know how to swim, especially in such deep water as this.

One man shouted that something had bitten him, while another yelled in pain, his scream cut dreadfully short as he was violently pulled under the surface. Tara heard a mass of bubbles rise, some poor soul's last breath seeking the surface he would never reach again. The boy became still and tried talking calmly over the hysterical shouts and cries of the men surrounding him.

"Reem, everyone, listen to me, stop struggling, take a deep breath and let yourself float on the water but of all things, remain still!" the boy advised; for Tara had learned a few useful survival skills during his time amongst the shadowmen.

Despite the boy's instructions, several of the soldiers were still in a state of panic; and in the span of a short few moments the many fearful voices soon became very few. Something hard bumped Tara's shoulder and he nervously reached out to see what it was. His hand felt a tall stony stalagmite, reaching up from the cold waters like a miniature island as their only refuge. The structure was smooth and slippery but at least it was something to hold on to. A long horrifying moment of silence followed while they were enveloped in the darkness.

"Is anyone there?" Tara pleaded. From the gloom, only a few faint whimpers met him in reply, "There's a rock here, come to my voice but try not to splash around, wade over slowly," the boy instructed. Soon, Tara felt a hand grasp at his shoulder, then another.

"Who's there?" it was Reem's voice.

"It's me," Tara replied

"Darg," another man answered.

"Jaffo," yet another whimpered.

"Arol," the last voice gurgled from the darkness while everyone was trying to keep afloat.

"Is there anyone else? Can you hear my voice ...speak if you can hear me," Reem whispered out loud, but only the sound of dripping water and their own fearful breaths broke the silence.

"Only three men?" Reem related sourly, "Tara, what

happened, how do we get out of this?" In the dark, no one saw the grim look of despair on the boy's face.

"I've never seen the floor do anything like that before," he declared.

"You may have walked over traps like that many times before, but you simply weren't heavy enough to trigger them as we did," Reem expressed coldly, "we have to get some light to see where we are."

"No chance of that, sir. We have torches strapped to our backs, but they're soaked through. There's no way they will light!" Arol stated out loud, the smugness of his tone was ripe with added anguish the others shared.

"Get a hold of yourself and keep your voice down," Reem ordered, "…as the boy warned us before, these water-beasts are attracted to movement and sound," their captain launched back.

"And also sources of light," Tara intervened with a whisper. This did present a problem, if they did manage to get a wet torch to catch aflame, whoever was holding it would be offering himself as fish food. Something grazed Jaffo's back and he let out a yelp.

"*Be quiet*!" Reem stressed through gritted teeth.

The object touched Jaffo again, lightly this time. He reached out with twitching fingers. It was one of their flasks floating on the surface, still corked. He laughed so giddily, the rest of the men would have eyed each other with a raised brow if they had been able to see.

The oil flask was only half full of fuel and puffed with air, which was probably the reason it hadn't sunk to the bottom. Reem untied two of his torches and carefully poured the fresh fuel onto them. It was very difficult to strike a flint while keeping oneself afloat, so they braced one man up while he attempted to light the torches in the dark. It took several aggravating moments, but they managed to get a frail flicker to catch as it slowly began to reveal the chamber. Reem nervously glanced around in the dim light while holding one torch above the other to help the bindings dry.

As the weak flame began to grow, its warm illumination reached the outer walls. It appeared that they were now trapped in a narrow well. There were tall sheer walls enclosing them on all sides, its ceiling was lost among the thick shadows above. The actual size of the room was fairly small, and Tara could see the chute they had dropped in from, which sat several dozen feet above their heads. Looking around, he found a symbol just breaking above the top of the waterline and the boy recognized it as a passage marker.

Surrounding them were more oil flasks, water skins and other loose items that were light enough to float, for apparently, all of the metal lamps they had brought along had sunk to the murky bottom. There were also a few still bodies of their fellow soldiers skimming the water, face down; which testified to their fate. To their horror, a thick pale body of a serpent broke the surface a mere arms-length from them, and disappeared just as suddenly under the glittering black pool as it dragged one of the buoyant corpses below to its watery lair. Upon seeing this, everyone suddenly froze in fear.

"There is a passage under there," Tara exclaimed, pointing at the carved symbols.

"Everyone grab what you can, especially the oil canteens, we need those the most," Reem grunted in earnest. Nobody liked the idea of wading out to grab bobbing items among the floating bodies with that giant creature lurking about.

"We've got no choice but to swim through the tunnel," Tara insisted.

"Are you kidding? Go underwater with that monster waiting for us; we just got our torches lit!" Darg barked quietly, "I'm not going under there; we'll all drown!"

Tara realized the frightened soldier wasn't far off from the sobering truth about their dire situation. He had heard about how the water level rises through the length of day cycle and drops dramatically during the nightfall season for reasons not understood. If they swam down there entirely blind, it just might come to a dead end; at least while they were trapped in the well they had a measure of light to comfort them.

"We can try to re-ignite the torches with more oil," Tara relayed.

"The boy is crazy!" Darg protested.

"If we move, we'll be eaten alive anyways, I say we stay here and wait for the others to rescue us," Jaffo suggested in hope, although a pin of doubt stifled his voice. Arol himself, remained silent from the argument, looking towards his captain for guidance.

"Even if the rest of our men came down to retrieve us, they would just fall into the same trap we did. Besides, they don't have enough rope to get us out of here; it has all been strapped together on the line anchored to the surface," Reem debated.

"But those two men you left behind can come get us," Darg suggested.

"And just how are they going to prop open a ton of stone, and lift us out of here without any rope?" Reem questioned the man's preposterous remark. Tara was frowning to himself, for despite all of his careful consideration and planning it was obvious now that they had come ill-prepared for this venture.

Through all the hushed bickering, Tara noticed something that had eluded him before. He could now see the entire symbol above the passageway. The water level was slowly sinking! Putting his lips to the water and noticing that it tasted slightly salty, the boy deduced that it might connect through the underwater channels to the Eon Sea. This well could be affected by the water pressure from the nearby geysers, for he had seen this happen before. The water level would sink, very much so. He pointed this out to the others.

They tried to dry their remaining torches above the flames of the others, and they lit their precious reserves as the bindings quickly burned away. Their small party quietly floated there, watching and waiting as the passageway slowly emerged through the murky water until it was halfway exposed. Only then did they dare to make their move. One by one, they waded over to the tunnel and caught the floor of the open hallway, although the water was waist high, at least they now had a measure of solid ground beneath their feet.

Darg was the last one to cross from their meager island over to the passage entrance. He paddled along with one arm, a torch in the other; but as he reached for the ledge something large and ghostly white wrapped him in its coils. He let out a hideous scream as a broad head filled with a thousand sharp teeth abruptly silenced him. His lifeless hand dropped the flaming torch it held as his headless body was trapped within a score of constricting coils that slithered about his corpse.

After their fall from the chute above, all the sinking lamps had slowly leaked their fuel, no one had noticed the glossy layer of oil floating on the surface of the pool.

Gazing back helplessly at the entwined soldier, the room behind them exploded into flames as the oil slick came in contact with the soldier's fallen torch. A stream of fire raced out to them along the surface of the water, licking forward into the passage as they turned to flee.

The boy, including Jaffo and Reem, had the sense to duck under the water, but Arol was badly burned before he too was pulled under the surface. The burst of fire had only lasted a moment as the fuel was exhausted, but at least the creature was nowhere in sight. The two guardsmen dragged their injured comrade down the hall to safety as the water continued to slowly drain away.

The passage ended in a huge mud-lined room; the water they waded through was now only a little more than ankle deep within this raised chamber. Here and there, strange fish of different shapes and sizes flopped about on the floor. Smaller fish darted around their feet and into the receding water of the passageway. They had breached a large room which appeared to be some sort of shrine. The ceiling was noticeably much higher here, as their poor flickering light could hardly reach the gloomy shadows above. The stale air within the room reeked of rancid meat, and they hurried to search the surrounding walls for another exit while choking on the stench.

Arol was severely crippled from his injuries, so they sat him down so he could lean against the wall near the portal to rest. Tara hurried off to investigate some interesting pillars at the far end of the room while the others searched the dark corners for signs of a way out. He discovered the entire back wall of the chamber was decorated with deep horizontal grooves that led up into the darkness above. There, he found a strange stumpy idol of polished translucent stone, which sat alone in the middle of a round pedestal, staring blindly upwards with its glossy eyes.

It wasn't long thereafter that the remaining water receded and drained from the room. Tara called to the others who had split up to search the area but they had found no other doorways. Out of the darkness there came a dull thud from the far wall, which was followed by a faint gurgling cry. Jaffo rushed back to get Arol, only to find a strange sight. What looked to be a small stalactite had impaled Arol through where he lay. Long sticklike legs had emerged from its broken edge and were firmly grasped to the man's head, while several little beaks were gnawing away at his distorted face. A stream of blood found its way to the wet floor, coloring the scene in a vivid red.

Jaffo gasped as Captain Reem approached him from behind and pulled him away, but not before he thrust his long knife down into the soft area above the shell; avenging his fallen comrade. The thing shrieked and shivered, unable to free its shell from the corpse, until it gave a final twitch and lay as still as stone while a thick black ooze seeped from the open gash left by the captain's blade. They retreated to where Tara stood near the short jade statue.

"Arol, is dead," the captain sighed as Tara looked away in remorse.

"Did you find any passages?" the boy asked with hope, but both men shook their heads in denial, "Then this seems like our only way out of this chamber," he gestured to the ribbed wall and turned his head upward.

They mentioned what kind of creature had killed their wounded companion as Tara glanced up nervously at the high ceiling in response. Handing his torch to Reem to remove the glare of its light, he motioned for him to step further away and took another look as his eyes adjusted to the dark.

He glimpsed something, a faint glow lighting the wide shaft walls far above, stationed directly over the idol. If they could manage to scale these walls, there must be a passage above they could reach. With mild regret, both soldiers dropped their torches on the floor to be left behind as they began their ascent up the sculpted walls.

This was going to be a difficult climb, and honestly, Tara didn't think he had the strength for it, but after a few moments, old familiar muscles started to kick in. The many bands he had been trapped underground had conditioned him to scale such steep terrain.

The ledges themselves became forgivingly deeper the higher they climbed, and soon they found themselves among the luminous moss growing near its apex. Jaffo and Reem touched these living sprouts curiously as the plants flared a bit brighter during the brief physical contact of their warm skin. At the top, they reached a small hole that led through into a winding tunnel, which branched off into two different directions, while even those appeared to diverge into many others beyond. Tara reflected momentarily about the writings he had seen before they had been so rudely dunked into the dark well.

"This must be the drawing of the maze we saw in the mural," Tara elated, "the symbols alongside it must have referred to the area we passed below."

"Perhaps, but why would someone show you the safe passage back there only to drop you into a watery grave? More likely it had shown a way to certain death," Jaffo scoffed at the boy.

"I don't think you understand," Tara debated, turning

back around to face Jaffo in the cramped passage, "this entire area was once an enormous city. The salt water might have crept in from the sea long ago, and the pit we fell into was probably just a type of trap to thwart dangerous beasts that roam these caverns ...or maybe it was a secret escape route at one time."

The narrow tunnels were slick with moss and moist to the touch, but the air here seemed to get gradually warmer. Tara had only been privileged with a short glimpse of the map painting before they had all been plunged into the well. If he was mistaken about the trail, they could always backtrack. He pulled out a damp chalky shell from his pocket and marked the wall, a trick Lela had taught him.

They crawled through the tight tunnels with Jaffo between them, grumbling all the way, who was sure they were becoming ever more lost with every step they took. Having been accustomed to this dim light, Tara came to an abrupt halt just as he noticed the lichen was faintly brighter down one particular hall. The others stumbled along closely behind him.

"What is it, Tara?" Reem asked.

"The boy is lost, and contemplating what passage we should take to our certain death," Jaffo added, mockingly.

"No, I just noticed something ...this way," Tara retorted as he trotted off ahead and bade the men to follow. The ailing guard grudgingly complied while Reem took up the rear of the trail; they both blindly felt their way along the slick walls despite the sparse phosphorescent moss.

'What was that?' Tara thought to himself while hearing a faint hiss up ahead, then a smile crossed his cheeks as a soft wind caressed his face. Preoccupied in their misery, the others had failed to notice the slight breeze.

"What is it now?" Jaffo scoffed as he bumped into the lad, "Hey boy! Where are you going?" he cried fearfully as he heard Tara suddenly run off ahead, barely making out his silhouette as it disappeared down the dark passage. As Tara flew forward through the shaft he could sense the breeze was getting stronger and the tunnel brighter, ever so slightly. Turning around the last corner, he let out a shout of glee that echoed down through the hallway. However, upon hearing the boy's cries, Jaffo slumped to the floor in anguish.

"That's it, the boy has fallen into another pit. We're on our own now," he let out with a pitiful sigh. Reem grunted with contempt and stepped over where the guard was seated to follow the child, as Jaffo jumped up in earnest behind his commander, "Hey, where are you going?" he cried out nervously in pursuit.

Reem hopped out from the gloomy tunnel to stand beside Tara in the wash of light, as Jaffo came up panting from behind to join the pair moments later. Surrounding the three companions was a colossal grotto whispering with the gentle hiss of steaming geysers. In front of them along the far wall were the ruins of an ancient city delicately carved into the cavern walls. The impressive structure was bathed in sunlight filtering through a familiar rift in the ceiling high above, through which they could see the bright blue sky overhead. Jaffo knelt and kissed the ground at their feet, unashamed about his zealous antics while powdering soil upon his cheeks.

"Oh thank you Sun God, giver of life, for guiding our way," Jaffo whimpered in praise. The boy curled his brow in mild concern as he glanced down towards the kneeling soldier, then back over to Captain Reem.

"You entrust these men as city guards?" he asked

quietly with a note of apprehension.

"The almighty Elders of Te-Na, aren't too terribly picky when it comes to hiring men for their grunt work," Reem responded with a quirky expression flashing across his face, while notably, including himself in the insult.

Tara had finally located the last cavern the two children had used to escape this forgotten underworld. He showed them the icy pool where he and Lela had emerged before, knowing their wild story would be authenticated. Now he knew what lay beyond the dark tunnels they had not taken the time to investigate before. While Jaffo danced merrily in the warm shaft of sunlight streaming from above, with a sprinkle of humor, it was clear to the boy that subterranean living might not agree with most.

The boy continued to explain to Reem about the types of rocks and light crystals that lay in the hidden tunnels beyond, but the Captain just had to take his word for it since there were no signs of such exotic stones here.

They scaled their way back up the same route that the pair of youths had taken before during their escape from the subterranean grotto. Reem was a little worried that they wouldn't find the rest of their party waiting above, and that they would have to risk walking all the way back to the city by foot under the hot sun. However, his fears proved to be premature. Once they were back upon the surface, Captain Reem used a triad compass he had retained throughout their odyssey; the Commander pointed the direct route to the city and calculated where they had begun their journey. After climbing over several craggy knolls littered among the dusty hills, they eventually spotted the bright flags of their camp near the pit where they had first entered.

It wasn't long before they reached the others and quickly sent more men down to raise the stone slab so they may rescue the pair of soldiers they had left behind at the portal; whom were waiting impatiently below and understandably shaken at this point, since the last thing they had heard were the desperate screams of their comrades, followed by sudden silence after the slam of a heavy stone had echoed down the hallway.

After relating their tale to his troops in short order, Reem and Tara took to their tents to rest; exhausted as they were. However, Jaffo stayed up to mesmerize the other soldiers in his troop with exaggerated yarns of his heroic bravery, all while the captain and the boy slept. The sobering fact that merely a few of their party had returned alive from the mysterious underworld, only helped to support his tall tales.

They broke camp after the captain awoke. To Tara, the long journey back to the city seemed to drag on, as his thoughts were heavy since he knew Lela was awaiting his return. They had been quarreling just before he had left, and he was hoping she would be in a better mood once she knew they would be getting their treasured relics back. He mentioned his thoughts to Reem as they rode on with the city gates looming in sight.

"You are still a young lad, my boy; and I must concede that girl of yours is quite a catch. Come next cycle, and you'll have to beat men away with a stick if you want to keep her," Reem laughed. Tara just blushed, admitting to himself he was indeed very lucky to have met her, and conceded when Reem cut his thoughts short.

"You know what they say, time together helps to bring partners closer ...and after the adventure you two have been through, I think you might have a hard time losing her," he offered with a sly grin.

Tara was silent for a long moment as he lingered in deep thought, considering that even if she was still mad at him that at least he had come back in one piece. Granted, Lela was truly beautiful and witty, but why did she always have to be so damn outspoken! Tara turned away, his face showing the slightest flicker of a pout.

At that moment, a mischievous thought entered his head, while he turned and cast a brassy smile towards the Captain as they rode through the rusted city gates to the rising applause from the throng of citizens who had gathered in the streets to welcome their return. With tense expectation, Tara looked around but couldn't find Lela in the crowd. To his delight, he eventually spotted her waving to him from the deck of their balcony high above on the tower wall; and was glad to see a look of relief in her tearful eyes, betraying the mask of her hardened exterior. Tara quickly dismounted, and pushed his way through the crowd while he made his way to the central palace.

'I know,' he thought cleverly, grinning to himself all the while as he ran up the long winding stairs to greet her, '...I'll tell Lela I'm in love with her,' he professed to himself to gather his courage; and just as Lela began to vent and fuss about how idiotic he had been to run off like that down into those dark terrible caves, and how desperately worried she had been, he admitted his true feelings for her as he took her into his arms.

As he had hoped, that admission certainly dulled her temper ...at least for a short while.

About the Author

Michel Savage has been devoted to writing throughout his career. If one reads between the lines, they will find his novels revolve around the reminder that we are only borrowing our small place on this planet but for a brief period of time, and to take responsibility for the environment, for one another and all other living creatures with which we share this world. And in doing so, hopefully planting a seed in our conscience of the importance to preserve what is left of the wilds, our untainted woodlands, and ever-dwindling rain forests.

He has had the blessing of sharing his stories and artwork around the globe, which is a gift in itself, and would encourage others not to waste too much of their lives chasing someone else's dreams but to follow their own.

One of the most valuable lessons he has learned in his years is that there are far more important things in life than power and money, such as kindness, compassion, and consideration towards others.

...share that thought if you will.

Enter the Grey Forest

www.**GreyForest**.com

Also by
Michel Savage

Shadoworld – Veil of Shadows

Ash was an orphaned street urchin who grew up in the gutters of a desolate medieval city; his bitter youth spent picking pockets and snatching trinkets from the wealthy to survive. Over the years his art for stealth and sharpened skills had drawn the attention of the Thieves Guild who took him into their folds. Little did they know that the boys tragic past would one day find itself woven within the treacherous schemes of a mysterious spider cult.

As of late, a series of chilling murders had befallen several nobles within the privileged upper districts. Their gruesome deaths had appeared to be centered around an ancient cursed skull, which had recently found its way into the hands of a rich collector. There were few who would trespass upon the strange realms of witchcraft and dark magic ...but a master thief does not fear those who dwell in darkness, for he is one with the shadows.

Shadoworld – Shadows Gate

Asra found himself alone in the middle of the barren sands, unable to remember who he was or how he had gotten there. Saved by a caravan of traveling gypsies, he entered into an exotic world of dancing acrobats, fortune tellers, and mystics who performed their skills for cheering crowds across the desert empires. However, his destiny would change the day he stumbled upon a forbidden shrine to find a mythical creature entombed beneath its shattered ruins.

Promises were whispered and a dark pact was made with the ancient demon; a bond of magic that would lead him on a perilous journey to reveal his forgotten past.

Outlaws of Europa

The 2nd moon of Jupiter has been turned into a prison planet. Where for several generations, robot drone ships have been dumping the scum of the universe and are patrolled by a ring of advanced security satellites that would destroy any vessel attempting to land. After a century of research, old core samples from the ice reveal that the frozen oceans of Europa hold the base element of an immortality drug that can extend the human lifespan several-fold. Now greedy military corporations race for the new fountain of youth, only to discover they can't disable the orbiting sentry which was programmed to protect itself at all costs.

It appears the Confederation has a problem. How do they get past a self-evolving AI that has appointed itself as Warden, and furthermore, retake a planet roaming with Earth's worst criminals who might well be immortal themselves.

Hellbot – Battle Planet

Tranquility was one of those out of the way planets in a system far out of reach from the normal space lanes. Loners, dreamers ...whoever they were, chose to colonize this world. Thirty cycles ago something went terribly wrong. It was rumored their terraformer reactor went critical, and few escaped the chain reaction that clouded the atmosphere with a planet-wide sand storm. A decade of hard labor evaporated overnight. What wasn't buried under the ocean of sand was left to fry under the twin suns. Human explorers began to wander back into the forgotten zone. No one knew of the machines that had evolved, or the war that raged beyond the edge of the universe ...where mankind did not belong.

Project EVE

In the late 1940s after the 2nd World War, a classified government program was created in order to explore the military use of psychics to gain an advantage for their soldiers during armed conflict. At a remote laboratory in the mountains, a secret compound comprised of several hundred test subjects were trained to enhance their abilities with the goal of achieving the skills of telepathy and mind control.

Assigned to investigate this covert project, Walter Grant found himself entangled in a web of conspiracy and deceit when he discovered that the residents of the colony were being held captive by the scientists who had hidden the ugly truth behind their dangerous experiments.

At the heart of the project was a girl named Eve, whose extraordinary mind held the key, a child who would prove to them why humanity could not handle such power.

Broken Mirror - Apophis 2029

Hurtling through space was an enormous tumbling rock known as MN4 our astronomers affectionately named after an ancient Egyptian god of destruction. Asteroid Apophis was the talk of the year that every scientific community on Earth was aware of, though its flyby in April 2029 was to be nothing more than a spectacular celestial event; but as warring nations were locked in global conflict, our civilization was unprepared for the devastation that followed in its wake.

Several years after governments fell and society dissolved a ragged pack of survivors stumble upon the buried truth, revealing what circumstances had led to the aftermath that ensued; leaving them to question their struggle to salvage what few splintered shards were left of our world that would forever define our bitter legacy.

Forgotten Future

At the edge of the world an impossible relic from the fables of antiquity has risen from the frozen wastelands of Antarctica. Professor Logan and his exploration team rush to investigate this historic find, but this unique discovery puts their lives in peril when they unearth the remnants of a long forgotten civilization left buried beneath the ice.

Within the twisting labyrinths below the melting glaciers they uncover an ancient culture which had perished from a mysterious cataclysm. They soon realize it was a polar shift which had caused their destruction, and our world was presently facing the same fate.

Witchwood - The Harvesting

Every day around the world hundreds of people go missing without a trace. Year after year, their numbers add up to millions of lost souls who are never to be seen again; and their numbers keep climbing ...this is where many of them went.

7 - The Fall

A strange and unexplained phenomenon led to the fall of civilization. It began on an evening like any other. The Sun had set on another day, but by the next morning, humanity realized that there were no more stars in the sky. Somehow, overnight, mankind had become alone in the universe and only an AI program knew why.

The Faerylands Trilogy

Faerylands I
The Grey Forest

Long, long ago the Faerie had roamed free, but for countless centuries now the fey themselves have remained unseen; hidden and withdrawn, shrouded within the boundaries of the Evermore. But just how they became imprisoned there was a mystery their own elders had forgotten or refused to speak of, and a subject of taboo among the ancients.

The Elvenborn had become a dying race, and now a strange and dreadful blight was encroaching upon their sanctuary. Ivy knew there was something terribly wrong with her world, something unspeakable her kind was hiding from. The Faerylands were vanishing, and she had to find out why.

Faerylands II
Soulstorm Keep

Many centuries after the passing of mankind, the blight known as the Craven still lingered, lurking within the shadows; a dark hunger awaiting its chance to consume what little was left of their fragile world. Only one among the Elves knew the true face of their enemy, with the knowledge to awaken the Undying and save the Faerylands before the living veil of the Evermore was forever lost.

Ivy Elvenborn was presented with an impossible quest - one that would take her on a distant journey to the Tower of Madness to seek the guidance of an ancient relic guarded within; but it would lead her to trespass beyond the gates of a forgotten castle; a ghostly fortress of despair where no living Faerie had ever tread. If she failed in her task, the entire race of Fey would be the last of their kind.

Faerylands III
Sorrowblade

Untold ages ago the race of Elves were cast to the four winds, forced to dwell in the underworld within the veil of the Evermore to protect the Tree of Life. Split into separate clans, their dying race withdrew to the far reaches of the world. There also existed a darker faction of Elves which had burrowed deep into the depths of the earth, evolving into the seven houses of the Drow. From the seed of the Elders came the children of the Faerie with a dire legacy to fulfill; a generation of Elvenborn whose destiny was to save the Faerylands.

Almost forgotten among the Fey were the whispered legends of a warrior priestess from the Sisterhood of Blood; a young outcast trained in the forbidden sorcery of an accursed cult known as the Obsidian Order. These maidens skilled in both spell and blade were charged with battling the dark and terrible blight known as the Craven which infested their world. This is their saga, for without their noble sacrifice all hope was lost.

Artwork from the Faerylands series
available online

Enter the Grey Forest

www.**GreyForest**.com